The Noonday Friends

The
Noonday Friends

By Mary Stolz

📚 HarperTrophy
A Division of HarperCollinsPublishers

Ce livre est pour mes deux chers amis,

Gladys Kellogg

et

Myron

Chapter One

Wishing it were cooler and wishing she weren't hungry, Franny Davis stood in line at the school cafeteria door, fingering the lunch pass in her sweater pocket. It was too warm today for her red sweater, but she was wearing it anyway, and though it was not really one of those wonderful bulky sweaters you saw in the advertisements, it looked like one. Sort of. Anyway, it was the only piece of clothing she owned that she liked. Her skirt was much mended and let down now as far as it was going to go. Of course all the girls were wearing short skirts these days, but there was a difference between short skirts that were bought that way—like the one Lila Wembleton had on—and short skirts that had gotten that way. You wouldn't think the difference would show, but somehow it did.

She got inside the door, showed her ticket to the teacher at the desk there, who glanced at it, then nodded and smiled encouragingly at Franny.

As if to make *up* for something, Franny thought touchily. Still, she smiled back. Every day she thought how nice it would be to say to that teacher, "Here, please give this to some child who needs it" —handing the ticket over with a gracious smile. "I find I am not in the least hungry today." Or "I find I won't be needing this anymore." But she never did hand it over with a gracious smile, because by noontime she *was* in the least hungry. Every noontime.

Soup (vegetable), sandwich (peanut butter), jello (lime), cookie (oatmeal), and milk. She went along the line, only half hearing the din and clatter of the vast room.

What she would have liked was to carry her lunch to school. Best of all, in a little lunch box with scenes painted on it. But she would have settled for a paper bag. Just so she carried it. Lila Wembleton had a plastic lunch box woven to look like a basket. It had shells pasted on it and was blue. Lila never had a free lunch pass.

Franny and her twin brother Jim nearly always had them, and it didn't bother Jim at all. He said it didn't bother him, and Jim usually said what he meant. He also said some things he didn't mean. Franny could see him now in a far corner of the cafeteria, standing at a table talking to a bunch of his friends, who were looking up at him and laughing. Through the noise of the lunch hour Franny couldn't make out a word, but she knew he'd be telling some wildness that people—especially boys —always half believed. Probably because they wanted to. Jim's stories were gory most of the time, full of sinister grown-ups who got duped and outwitted by boys.

But he doesn't mind anything, Franny thought now, standing motionless, tray in hand. Not the free lunch ticket or his awful-looking clothes or the way Papa never keeps a job or *anything*.

I don't understand boys, Franny thought to herself, and started nervously as a boy's voice behind her said, "Move on, dopus. You wanna block the whole line?"

Franny moved off without looking back. She searched for a place to sit.

"Franny! Franny! Over here!"

Franny smiled with relief and went to sit beside Simone Orgella.

"Oh, my," said Simone, giving a great happy sigh and waving her slender arms. "Did you see that pretty new art teacher we have? Her name is Miss Rose. Do you have her?"

"I don't get art until next week."

"Franny, she's as pretty as a—as a rose. She's so pretty she makes my head ache."

Franny nodded. Whenever Simone saw something she found very beautiful, she got a headache, or a stomachache. It was a peculiar way to be, but Simone's way just the same.

"Do you suppose her first name could be Rose too?" Simone said. "Rose Rose. That would be nice."

"How about Rosie?"

Simone ignored that. "What I want is for everyone to be pretty, and I only want to look at pretty things and pretty people, all the time."

"I know," said Franny. "You've already said."

Simone herself was pretty. Very. She had a fly-away fragile air and the most wonderful eyes Franny had ever seen. Simone had seven brothers and sisters, a grandmother, and her parents, and they all had these dark sparkling eyes with long fringy lashes black as soot. Franny, who allowed herself to dream impossible things, sometimes dreamed that her own eyes had suddenly become heavily blackly fringed and dark as coffee. She had another dream about becoming a mermaid. When she'd been smaller, she'd really thought there might just be a way to do it, if

4 ❋

she could find the right spell to say, encounter the right witch. Now she only thought how marvelous it would be, the way Simone thought about becoming a child TV actress.

"My cousin Francisco is coming up from San Juan to stay with us," said Simone, nibbling at her cookie, taking a long time with it. "Tomorrow he gets here."

Golly, thought Franny. I wonder where he's going to sleep. She didn't ask. People in this neighborhood always found room for another relative, another baby.

"What I think," she said to Simone, "is why leave San Juan? I mean, if it's as beautiful as you say and all."

"Oh, it is," said Simone, who'd been born in Manhattan and never been out of it. "Gorgeous. The sun shines all the time, and you can swim in the ocean every day of the year, and they have flowers everywhere. Flowers big as a baby's head."

"Then why leave?" Franny insisted.

"Francisco says he wants to get ahead."

"Can't he get ahead in San Juan?"

Simone moved restlessly. "Franny, do you always have to be so picky?"

"I wasn't being picky, I was only asking—"

She broke off because Simone had begun to call a greeting and then stopped short, her face clouding. Franny twisted around to look.

Lila Wembleton, carrying her pretty lunch box,

stood at the doorway. She looked for a moment at Simone and Franny, then lifted her chin and turned away.

"What's the matter with her?" Franny asked.

"Who cares? The noisy thing."

"I thought she was your friend," Franny said coldly.

Simone hesitated. "Well, I can have a noisy friend, can't I?" she said finally.

Franny laughed at that, but Simone went right on looking cross.

"Do you know what she did yesterday? We were playing hopscotch in front of her house and I was beating. I always beat. Even if she does take dancing lessons, Lila is clumsy. So all of a sudden she got mad and told me to go away." Simone's voice lifted in mimicry. " 'You just beat it, Simone, you hear? This is my property!' "

Franny blinked. "Her property? The sidewalk?"

"Her father," Simone said in a low, impressive tone, "owns that whole building that they live in, himself."

"He does?" Franny couldn't imagine such a thing. Owning a building? Lila Wembleton's father? She felt a sharp stab of envy. So Lila Wembleton was rich. She took dancing lessons and carried her lunch to school and had pretty clothes and there'd be no way ever to get the best of her because she was rich.

Mr. Davis said, pretty often, sounding as if he

meant it, that money was unimportant, that the only thing it had to do with character was to destroy it. Franny had been willing to accept that because she'd never personally known anyone who had any money before. But Lila Wembleton was her enemy, and finding out that her father wasn't a poor man, like most people's fathers, made her more to be feared than ever.

Franny didn't have a lot of friends the way her brother Jim did. Since Martha Piermont had moved to someplace in Long Island, her only real friend was Simone, because after school and on weekends Franny had to take care of her little brother, and the fact was most girls didn't want your little brother trailing you all over the place.

But Lila Wembleton—she didn't have any brothers or sisters, and Franny would have bet anything she didn't have to help her mother around the house.

"I don't believe it," she said suddenly.

"What don't you believe?"

"I don't believe Lila is rich. Why would they be living in this neighborhood? Why would she be going to this ratty old school? People who live around here aren't rich, that's all."

"Landlords would be, I suppose," Simone said indifferently. "I mean, if he owns his whole building—"

"What do you mean, if? You said he did."

"I mean, *since* he owns—" Simone waved her

hands impatiently. "Let's go outside, huh?"

There was no place left in any of the games that were going on in the crowded play yard, so Simone and Franny stood against a wall and watched the high-pitched activity of people determined to have fun in too little space and too little time.

Somewhere in the distance a siren began to moan. Franny and Simone walked over to the iron fence that separated the schoolyard from the street, waiting to see if it would be an ambulance or a police car.

"I hate ambulances," Simone said, shivering. "I hate to think about people dying. I mean, they cover their faces with sheets and then they're all alone and —oh, Franny, it must be awful."

Franny tried to close her ears. She tried never to think about—she didn't even like the word and wouldn't pronounce it in her mind. Mostly she tried never to think that maybe one day Papa or Mama— A shudder ran through her thin body, as she tried to force the thought away.

"I saw a dead cat once," Simone went on. "It looked horrible. It was lying there on the sidewalk and—"

"Don't!" Franny cried out. "Don't, Simone. I won't listen, I won't—"

An ambulance came down the street, scattering trucks and cars to either side, moving with what seemed to Franny a horrible swiftness and smooth-

ness. People on the sidewalk stopped to watch its passage, as they might stop for a parade, and a shiver of excitement seemed to pass over them.

"Boy, would I like to drive one of those things," said Jimmy Davis. "Would I ever."

Franny looked around and found her brother and his friends pressed against the fence, showing signs of disappointment. Probably, she thought, they'd been hoping for a police car chasing burglars down the street.

She stared after the disappearing ambulance. "I wonder where it's going," she said to her brother in a low voice.

"Now, don't start that, Franny," he said, moving away. "There's fifty thousand buildings around here, so there's no point in you always deciding right away that the ambulance is going to our house."

"Why should you think that?" Simone asked with surprise. "I mean, what a funny thing to think."

Franny wouldn't answer. But she gave her brother a cold look and he returned it uneasily. They both knew why she might be scared, why . . .

One time when an ambulance had streaked with its wailing smoothness past Franny and Jimmy, who were walking home from school, it *had* gone to their building. They had come around a corner to find it, gleaming and ominous, surrounded by a crowd of curious neighbors, right in front of their door.

Franny shut her eyes tightly now as if to squeeze

away the picture of that day, but it stayed before her like a strange moving picture . . . the two of them, her and Jimmy, turning that corner, stopping when they saw the ambulance so huge and still at the curb, then going forward, laughing nervously. All this time later—that had happened more than two years ago— Franny couldn't tell if they had really guessed why the ambulance was there. But it seemed to her now that they had, that they hadn't been surprised at all, only scared, awfully scared, when two men in white came out of the house carrying a stretcher with Mama walking beside it, her hand on Papa's shoulder, biting her lips and looking—scared too.

"It's all right, it's all right," she'd said to them in a high strange voice when they ran forward. "I tell you, it's all right. Papa's had a fainting spell, that's all. Go upstairs to Mrs. Mundy. She'll take care of you, she'll get your dinner, she'll—"

"Mama, I don't want to go up with Mrs. Mundy," Franny had yelled, the tears dashing down her cheeks. "I want to go with you and Papa."

"I said upstairs, Franny. Don't argue, just *go*."

When Mama got that tone in her voice, you didn't argue. She and Jimmy had gone into the building, because Mama wouldn't even let them wait and see the men put Papa in the ambulance.

"I hate her," Franny had said to herself, climbing the stairs, her knees shaking so that she almost thought she'd never get to the third floor at all. "I hate her," she'd burst out to Jimmy.

"Don't you dare say anything like that," he snarled, turning on her. "Don't you dare."

Suddenly overwhelmed, Franny sat down on the stairway and cried in earnest. She thought Jimmy had gone angrily on, but after a minute felt his hand on her shoulder, the way Mama had put her hand on Papa's, and he said, "Don't cry, Franny. It'll be all right. You heard what Mama said. Papa just had a fainting spell or something."

"Suppose he dies," she shrieked. "Jimmy, suppose Papa—"

"But he won't, I tell you!" Jimmy said loudly. "So you just stop that, Franny. Boy, some help you are to people. What do you want to do, scare Marshall to death?"

What he meant was, she was scaring the two of them, because Marshall wasn't even three yet, and when they got to Mrs. Mundy's apartment they found him eating ice cream and looking happy, because the Davis children hardly ever got ice cream.

Mrs. Mundy had even offered some to them, but she and Jimmy just shook their heads.

Papa had gotten better. He was in the hospital for nearly three months, and when he came home he was so thin, so quiet, so *different*. He couldn't go to work for a long time after that, and he and Mama were still trying to pay back the bills for his sickness. But he *had* gotten better, and started to get jobs again, and after a while wasn't so thin, and began to talk a lot, the way he used to.

But Franny could never hear a siren now without that flutter of fear, and for all his talk, she suspected Jimmy felt the same.

"Franny, are you listening to me? Franny Davis!"

"Oh, I'm sorry, Simone. I was thinking . . . that's all."

"I said, can you come home with me after school?"

Franny hesitated, shook her head.

"I'll let you hold the baby. And feed him."

Franny had a moment's yearning temptation. "I'll come on the weekend. If I can bring Marshall."

"You never can do anything except on weekends," Simone complained. "How can people be friends only on weekends?"

Franny felt a shock of alarm. "Well, for Pete's sake," she said. "There's lunchtime, isn't there? What are we doing now?"

"Big deal."

Stiffening, Franny said, "If you don't want to be friends, Simone, then all right." Threatened, as she so often was, with tears, Franny, as she usually did, fought them back. "See if I care," she said airily.

"I didn't say I didn't want to be friends. I said you can't ever do anything except on weekends. You don't have to get mad at me just because you're always busy most of the time."

"I didn't get mad at you because I'm always—"

Franny broke off, started again. "I mean, *I'm* not mad at *you*—" She stopped again, confused.

The truth was, she was busy just about all the time, and couldn't go to other girls' houses after school the way Simone and Lila and the others did. She had to get dinner started for her mother, who came in tired from the laundry where she worked until early in the evening. She had to get Marshall at Mrs. Mundy's. This year she had a lot of homework to do too. Where did people get the time to do anything except homework and housework?

"If you don't want to be friends," she said again in a thin high voice, "then all right. You have all these brothers and sisters and grandmothers and things helping each other all the time. But Marshall only has me."

"He could stay with Mrs. Mundy once in a while, couldn't he?"

"He only stays with her until three o'clock. She doesn't keep him after that, and you know it." The stinging behind her eyes continued, but she ignored it grandly. "Go be friends with dopey rich Lila. See if I care."

Simone, eyes flashing, hesitated at this repeated threat. Should she turn on her heel and walk away? Yes or no? They stared at each other, waiting to see what would happen. Then Simone laughed.

"I can't be friends with dopey rich Lila," she said. "Dopey rich Lila isn't talking to me."

Franny laughed too, and they went back to class arm in arm.

But that afternoon, when school was out and she was going home, half running because she had errands to do and the sky was beginning to cloud up, she wondered if maybe now Simone and Lila would be together anyway.

I should worry, I should care, I should marry a millionaire. . . .

She and Martha used to say that to people, shouting it at them sometimes. It was silly and in its silly way had made them feel better. Only she was older now, and saying something like that by yourself, to yourself, didn't make any sense.

In the supermarket all she had to buy was a can of red kidney beans and a half a pound of ground meat to stretch out the chili that Mama had made on Sunday. Tomorrow evening, Wednesday, was the time they did their week's marketing, and nearly always on Tuesday Franny had to get something to make dinner stretch.

She had an extra nickel and paused for a moment before the candy counter, wanting to get Marshall a surprise. But she walked on. To begin with, Mama hadn't said she could. And then the trouble with little children was that if you did something like that once, the next time they expected it. They never seemed to remember that once they *had* had a surprise, they only noticed that now they *weren't* having one.

"It's going to rain," said a woman in front of her as they came out of the market. "What do you think of that? Sunny one minute, pouring the next." She sounded furious.

The sky was very dark now, and as Franny ran down the street toward her apartment building the rain began to fall heavily. In a moment sidewalks and streets were drenched. She encountered Jimmy, racing toward her from the opposite direction, and they arrived in the vestibule together, breathless from the effort to keep their feet from getting wet. The Davises had only one pair of shoes apiece, and they always ran when it rained.

"Consarnit," Jimmy said loudly. "Golblamit."

Franny said nothing. He was angry because he couldn't stay out and play stickball with his friends, but it was no lookout of hers. And her feet were wet too.

Chapter Two

During the week Marshall spent the day across the hall with Mrs. Mundy, their neighbor, while his father and mother were working and the twins were at school.

Marshall liked Mrs. Mundy. But not very much. Not all of the time. She was long and thin and stiff. Marshall, looking up at her from his low height, sometimes thought she looked like a telephone pole with a face. He had told this to Franny once. She giggled and then told him he must never say it again.

"You wouldn't want to hurt her feelings," she said.

Marshall wasn't sure. Sometimes Mrs. Mundy hurt his feelings. He stuck out his lip.

"Well, then," Franny said, "you wouldn't want to be like Jimmy, would you? *Blurting* things?"

Marshall shook his head. He did not at all want to be like Jim. Jimmy, their father said, blurted out anything that came into his head. Once Jim had looked right at Mrs. Mundy and said, "Why do you have those four hairs growing out of your chin?" Everybody had gotten very excited, and Mrs. Davis made Jimmy apologize. No, Marshall decided, he didn't want to blurt or be like Jimmy.

"Okay," he'd told Franny. Anyway, once he had told his sister something, he usually felt it was all told. Of course he told his parents lots of things. But it wasn't the same as with Franny, who played games and taught him things and wasn't tall and never scolded.

Now he was in Mrs. Mundy's kitchen, doing one of the things Franny had taught him. He was telling time. Or, actually, waiting until the hands of the clock got in a position where he could tell the time. When the big hand got to twelve, and the little hand got to three, that meant it was three o'clock, so he could leave and go across the hall to wait for Franny.

Franny had taught Marshall how to tell when it was three o'clock and was teaching him the rest of the hours too. After a while she was going to teach him the times in between the hours, but Marshall could already see that that was going to be harder. She had taught him how to tie his shoelaces, how to write numbers up to ten, letters as far as *I,* how to make instant pudding and instant fudge. She wouldn't let him cook anything where he had to use the stove yet, but Marshall was confident that he would come to that, too, in time.

Mrs. Mundy clumped from the sink to the stove. She was getting her dinner ready. She always got it all prepared early in the afternoon while Marshall was still with her. Then when he'd gone to meet Franny at the head of the stairs, she lay down. She never said that Marshall made her tired, but he suspected he did.

Marshall took his attention from the clock and gave it to the dinner preparations.

"You're going to have two nice little chops and some tomatoes and some onions," he informed her. Mrs. Mundy nodded. "And a baked potato," Marshall added.

"That's right."

"What will you have for dessert?"

"Ice cream and gingerbread."

"Oh." Marshall sighed. He had lunch every day with Mrs. Mundy, but they never had ice cream and gingerbread. At least, he'd had ice cream once, but a long time ago and now he couldn't remember why.

"It's raining," said Mrs. Mundy, changing the subject. "What do you know."

Marshall looked at the window and saw that it was raining, all right. He looked at the clock.

"I have to go now," he said. "Thank you for the nice day." His mother had told him to say that every afternoon when he left.

"Suppose it wasn't a nice day?" he had asked.

"Say it anyway," Mrs. Davis had told him. "Mrs. Mundy tries to make all your days nice."

Marshall wasn't altogether sure of this but generally did what he was told.

He didn't know whether Mrs. Mundy heard him or not. She just said, as she always did, "All right, Marshall. Run along."

He ran along.

At the top of the dark stairway he waited impatiently, twining his leg around the banister. The rain was coming down harder. It beat on the skylight above him, and once or twice thunder rumbled out there in the city.

Marshall waited.

And now here came Franny, running up the stairs, her red sweater flying, blonde hair flopping. Marshall brightened, then scowled as he spied Jim mounting the stairs immediately behind his sister.

"Hiya, Smiley," said Jim. "Who gave you the black eye?"

"What black—" Marshall began, then snapped

his mouth shut as Jim let out a hoot of laughter. "Boy, are you funny," Marshall muttered. "Are you ever funny."

"Hope to tell you," said Jim cheerfully. He opened their apartment door. "This way to the Black Hole of Calcutta, folks. Mind the scorpions, the bats, and the human sacrifices. Just a moment while I get this flare going—"

Franny snapped on the wall light. It only encouraged Jimmy if you replied to his nonsense, so she ignored him. It was true that their apartment wasn't a bright place. It faced the courtyard and backed up almost right against a tall building on the next street. Today they went around and put on the lights everywhere.

Over in one corner was a small chair with a tray across the arms and a pad and pencil on the tray. This was Marshall's school, but he and Franny never played school when Jimmy was home. Now Franny went into the kitchen and Jim slouched in their father's chair.

"You do anything exciting today?" he asked his younger brother.

Marshall thought back, shook his head. "Did you?"

Jimmy had been sent to the principal's office for putting his finger on the fountain spigot in the hallway, but this wasn't the sort of excitement he shared with his family if he could help it.

"Nothing much," he said. "I got waylaid on the

way home by a band of Mexican desperadoes, but it wasn't anything I couldn't handle."

"You fended them off," said Marshall. He knew the words because Jimmy used them so often.

"Yup. I fended them off."

"What with?"

"My three-color ballpoint pen. I fended them off with the red and then fended them off with the blue. They fled before I got to green."

"What was a band of Mexican desperadoes doing here anyway?" Franny asked from the kitchen.

"Up for the World's Fair," Jim explained, and looked pleased when the other two laughed. Most of the time he was in trouble of one kind or another with them, and he now proceeded to get into it again.

Marshall had lost interest in the conversation and had fallen into a moody contemplation of their cat Fudge, who was on the windowsill watching the rain. It went past the window, falling to the gray areaway below like thousands of wet strings. Now and then Fudge put a paw against the pane as a large drop ran jerkily down the glass.

Marshall tried to figure what could be in the cat's mind. Did he think that was a tiny wet mouse running down the window out there? Did he think it was a silver thread meant for him to play with? Sometimes Marshall put a bit of paper on the end of a string and dragged it around for Fudge to chase.

Maybe he thought someone out there was trying to play with him that way.

"What do you suppose Fudge is thinking about?" he asked Jim.

"Food. That's all he ever thinks about."

"How do you know that?" Marshall said indignantly.

"I just know."

"Well, you can't just know."

"What is he thinking about then, smarty?"

"Maybe that somebody's out there on the other side of the window trying to play with him."

"Boy, if that isn't a babyish idea," said Jim. "Boy."

"You just wait till I grow up," Marshall said threateningly.

Jim didn't ask what would happen. He just said, "Okay. I'll wait."

"You just wait and see!"

"Okay. I'll wait and see."

Since he wouldn't ask, Marshall told him what was going to happen. "You just wait and see, Jim. When I grow up, I'll bop you!"

"You and who else?"

"Me and just me!" Marshall yelled.

"Hah," said Jim, giving a scornful smile. "Any bopping gets done in this family, let me tell you, it'll be me bopping you, all right. You couldn't bop a biscuit, you baby."

"I don't want to bop a biscuit," Marshall said furiously. He jumped up and down with rage. "I want to bop you!"

"Well, you can't. Not unless I let you, and I won't do that. So just pipe down, baby boy."

Marshall started across the room, his fists raised. He was so angry he could hardly see. Suddenly the breath was knocked out of him and he was sitting on the floor in front of Jim. He hadn't even had a chance to start howling when Franny came into the room and knelt beside him.

"Now, honey," she said soothingly. "Now, Marsh. Did you fall down?"

"He knocked me down!" Marshall wailed, his breath returning. "He just took and knocked me down!"

"Why, you big bully," Franny said, turning on her twin, her eyes wide with wrath. Jim, who'd been starting to laugh, suddenly looked alarmed. He didn't want two of them after him at once.

"I didn't do a thing," he said. "Not a thing."

"Then why is he on the floor crying?" Franny demanded.

"Yes, why am I?" said Marshall, sniffling.

"My gosh—oh, boy. What a family. Look, he was coming across the room like a cannonball right at me, so I just put up my feet and he ran into them. I can't help it if dopes run into my feet, can I?"

"Did you have to put your feet up?" said Franny. "You must have known he'd run into them."

24

"Well, of course I knew," Jim said loudly. "What was I supposed to do? Sit here and let him crash right into me? He might have broken my tooth or something. I gotta protect myself, don't I?"

"Protect yourself," Franny said haughtily. "You should be ashamed. Picking on a baby."

"I am not a baby!" Marshall yelled. "Don't you dare to call me a baby!"

"Yeah, where do you get off, calling him a baby?" Jim demanded. "He's going to be five years old pretty soon, and going to school and all. You better watch the way you talk, Franny."

Marshall looked at his brother suspiciously, but Jim seemed very serious and important, and all at once Marshall remembered that he *was* going to be five years old in—well, he didn't know when but pretty soon. He was going to have a birthday. A smile lit up his face and shone equally on his brother and sister here before him.

"That's going to be pretty nice, isn't it?" he asked. "I'm going to have a party and a cake and lots of presents and—"

Franny and Jim exchanged uneasy glances.

"Well, you know now, Marsh," Jim began, "sometimes it doesn't work out that way. I mean people don't *always* have parties."

"Oh, no," Marshall said with calm and happy certainty. "People always do. Parties and cakes and lots of presents and—lots of things."

"Now, Marshall, try to think back," Franny said.

"When Jimmy and I had our birthday in April, remember, *we* didn't have a party. We went to the movies, and we each got a sweater."

Marshall thought back. "You had a cake," he said. "With writing on it in icing that Mama made."

"Yes, we did," Franny said eagerly. "A lovely cake and everything. Who wants a party besides that?"

"I do," said Marshall.

"Well, so does everybody," Jim snapped. "You think you're the only one wants—"

"You didn't," Marshall interrupted. He was still thinking back. "You *said*. Parties are only for babies, that's what you said. I guess," he added thoughtfully, "I am sort of a baby. About some things," he added, wanting to be quite clear.

"That's what they told us to say," Jim exploded. "That—"

Franny suddenly burst into song. She went spinning about the room in a wild singing dance. The surprise of it cut off Jim's words and drove the thought even of his birthday from Marshall's mind.

"What are you doing, Franny?" Jim demanded. "Are you crazy or something?"

"Crazy? Because I feel like dancing and singing? *Tra-la-la, tra-la-la* . . ." Franny waved her arms and her long thin legs and sang at the top of her high thin voice. "I am not crazy, brother dear. I am born to sing and dance," she caroled. "Like a bird on the wing, I dance and I sing . . ."

"Oh, for Pete's sake," Jim muttered.

But Marshall stared, entranced. He thought his sister simply wonderful. He started to spin, too, around and around, as fast as he could, until the room reeled past him crazily and at length he staggered to the big chair and collapsed in it, his head whirling.

Franny subsided in a graceful curtsy. "I hope your Majesty is pleased with my poor performance," she said.

Marshall waved his hand airily. "My Majesty is pleased as Punch." He lurched from one arm of the chair to the other, trying to look like a top running down, because that was how he felt.

Franny began to chant. "Punch and Bunch sat down to lunch, munch, crunch—"

"Blunch . . . glunch!" yelled Marshall.

"If you want my opinion," growled Jim, "you're both missing most of your marbles."

"Do you want his opinion, Marsh?" said Franny.

Marshall shook his head. It was hardly reeling at all now.

"Neither do I," said Franny to Jim. "So I'm afraid you'll just have to take it back. Do try to put it to some good use."

"Oh, I'm going out," Jim said, stamping to the closet. "When you two get in this mood, you drive me batty." He burrowed around, came up with his box of baseball trading cards.

"Jim!" Franny said bossily. "You can't go out, hear? You'll get your shoes wet and you'll catch cold and then we'll all catch it from you. You stay right here till Mama gets home, do you hear?"

Jim turned at the apartment door. "Phooey," he said, and went out.

"Oh, my gosh," Franny mourned. "Mama will be furious."

"Mama will be furious, and Jimmy will be soaked," said Marshall. He looked at his sister with an expectant smile.

For a moment she hesitated, then she smiled too. "Let's see— Oh, I have it. *Mama will be furious, and Jimmy will be soaked, and we'll all catch pneumonia, the old frog croaked.*"

Marshall roared with laughter. He and Franny had lots of games, and this was one of his favorites. He never could think of a last line himself, but was pretty good at thinking up first lines. Franny *always* could finish up with a funny rhyme.

Chapter Three

When people asked the Davis children what their father did, they replied, "He's an artist," and what they said was true. Mr. Davis painted whenever he could, often when he should have been doing something else—like looking for a job or going to the one he had. And when he was painting, he forgot everything else in the world. This was sufficient to make him an artist.

He did not have a studio of his own but used a

corner of a loft belonging to a friend of his. His friend, Tulio, also an artist, had once sold a painting but that had been quite a while ago, and he had long since spent the money. So he couldn't afford to lend Mr. Davis either canvas or paint. All he could do was let him have an easel at one end of the loft, and Mr. Davis was grateful for that.

All this week, however, Mr. Davis had firmly marched past the building where the loft and his easel were. He had a job now, and he intended to keep it. He would paint, he told himself, only on Sundays, and then only when there was extra money for paint and canvas. There were, as he'd be the first to admit, many things to be bought first, many bills to be attended to.

There was the matter of shoes, for instance. Everyone in the family needed shoes. Mr. Davis figured that pretty soon he'd be able to get them. At a discount. His new job was in a shoe store. It wasn't a very good shoe store, and he wasn't a very good shoe salesman. But, he told himself, he could improve. And after he'd established himself, after he'd been there, say, a month, he could undoubtedly manage to get shoes for the entire family.

He climbed the stairs to the top floor, entered his apartment, and stood a moment in the doorway, looking at his wife and children. Why was there something so touching about shabbiness? Why did it move the heart in this sweet and painful fashion? His

31 �

wife, once an Irish beauty, had grown thin and sharp-featured, and still the beauty was there. As if the same woman had been painted by Renoir and then by Kollwitz. His children seemed all eyes and knobbly bones. He felt there was nothing, nothing he couldn't, wouldn't, do to make their lives brighter and better.

A man can make any job a success, he said to himself, make any job worthwhile. I will become a shoe salesman unequaled on Fourteenth Street, and then I will move my family to a huge sunny apartment where we will dine upon strawberries, sugar, and cream. In a manner of speaking, of course.

Mr. Davis often talked to himself this way. Not out loud, but in such a way that it occupied his full attention and prevented him from noticing what was going on around him, or even what he himself was doing.

For instance, he now entered his apartment, removed his wet shoes, let Franny take them from him, accepted with a smile his wife's evening kiss, gently lifted Fudge from the big chair and sat down in it, and all the time he was only listening to that voice, his own, in his head.

I will be a shoe salesman to pattern by. Who knows, one day I may even *own* a shoe store.

Instead of cheering him up, this brought on a sense of depression. It was not that he had anything against shoe stores. Only he didn't want to own one.

He wanted to paint pictures. Now, if he could somehow put aside a little of next week's salary and get a tube of zinc white, then if he squeezed hard there might be a bit left in those other tubes, and if so he could—

"What was that, Jimmy?" he interrupted himself, at last hearing a voice other than that in his mind. "What did you say?"

But Jim, who'd repeated himself twice, was annoyed and wouldn't speak.

"He's been trying to tell you," Franny said, "that he won the high jump at gym this afternoon."

"Why, that's great," said Mr. Davis. "Just great, Jim. That sort of muscular coordination and power is a splendid thing. I never did have it myself. To the day I left high school I regarded with awe any gymnastic equipment more complicated than a seesaw." He smiled at his son, who tried to go on frowning but failed.

When Mr. Davis smiled, few people could be cross with him. It was one of the reasons he didn't lose jobs sooner than he did. Of course in the end he always did lose them, because even a smile doesn't make up to employers for employees who forget to come to work or forget that they are at work when they get there. But Mr. Davis's smile, it was said, could charm a bird out of a tree. If they had lived where there were birds and trees, it might well have done so.

They did not. They lived in a section of the city

known as Greenwich Village, and to be sure there were both trees and birds in Washington Square, which was part of the Village, only not their part.

"Papa," Franny said now, "did you know that a girl in my class's father owns the whole building that they live in? She's the only rich person that I personally have ever known."

"Owning your own building in these parts doesn't necessarily mean that you're rich. Maybe you've got some old tenement that you can't get rid of. Being a landlord around here sounds to me like a good way to go broke fast."

It isn't one of the ways I've tried, he said to himself, and I've tried a few. But it seemed unlikely that anyone in these parts, sending his kid to that school, would be rich. Unless he was a tightwad. If I had money, thought Mr. Davis, I'd send the children to a good private progressive school. Well, when I really get cracking at this new job, it shouldn't be impossible.

"Say," he said, "how would you two like to go to a private school?"

Mrs. Davis opened her mouth to speak, shut it, got up, and went to the kitchen, closing the door on Jim's "Hey, boy, that'd be great. When do we start?"

"Well, it's this way," said Mr. Davis. "It seems that at last I've got in the way of a really good thing. This new job has opportunities, fine opportunities. It may be only a matter of time before . . ."

When the children went to bed, Franny, in her narrow cot by the wall, hardly thought at all about her father's suggestion. Like her own dream of becoming a mermaid, her father's dreams seemed to her reasonable and impossible at once. For herself, she wanted to go to school with Simone, with Mrs. Fedler as her homeroom teacher and Miss Roman as her gym teacher.

She wondered what Miss Rose would be like. Honestly, that Simone. If somebody was pretty, that was all Simone asked. Of course in a way that was nice, because it probably meant Franny herself was pretty. She didn't quite think so, but maybe it was true. She hoped Miss Rose would be something *besides* pretty, because next to geography, art was her favorite subject. Like her father, she loved color. Lots and lots of color....

Her eyes closed, opened again as she heard Marshall, in the bottom bunk under Jim, buzzing to himself. Pretending to be running a garage again, and probably planning to stay up all night. Marshall was always trying to stay up all night. He'd never made it yet, but he kept trying. What a funny, nice, dear little boy he—

Franny was asleep.

Jim flopped from one side to another, muttering, "G'wan, g'wan, ya dumb bunny. I'll spit in your eye and drown ya." Even in his dreams Jim was usually involved in violence. He was always getting into fights. Last time he'd been in Mr. Bradley's office, the principal had asked him why. "Why are you always fighting, Jim?" Mr. Bradley had asked. The only explanation that had occurred to Jim was "I like to fight." Somehow he didn't think that was the sort of answer Mr. Bradley had in mind, so he'd just shrugged and then said hastily, "I don't know, Mr. Bradley. Honest. It just—happens." Mr. Bradley was okay. Sort of snoopy, but in Jim's experience most adults except his parents were snoops. "Why do you make up these wild, fanciful tales?" Mr. Bradley had asked. "Do you realize that you frightened people, telling them that if they got too close to the cactus it would snap off their fingers?" Jim had smothered a laugh and said, "Didn't scare the guys." "Well," Mr. Bradley had said, "You did frighten some of the girls." "Girls'll believe anything," Jim had said. "All the more reason to keep from telling them alarming stories," said Mr. Bradley, which showed how much he knew about anything. Just before he'd fallen asleep, Jim had wondered how long it would take his father to get enough money to send them to a private school. That might be sort of good, starting over somewhere else. On the other hand, he really didn't mind it where he was. He sort of thought that when the time came, he'd tell his father, "That's okay, Pop. I guess I'll just stay where I am." So then they could use all that money for something else. Like maybe moving to a place where he could have his own room. Below him, Marshall had been beeping and buzzing steadily, driving his little toy cars around. Jim started to say, "Pipe down, baby boy," but fell asleep before he had a chance.

In the bottom bunk Marshall had made a garage and highways of the blankets and sheets. He was running his toy cars—he had two—in and out of the garage, up and down the highways. Now and then he'd stop and try to peer through the darkness. But he couldn't see anything. He liked the sound of the rain falling, and he liked this room and the cozy feeling of knowing his parents were just on the other side of the door. He liked having Fudge curled up asleep at the foot of the bed and knowing that Franny was in here. He was going to stay up all night. He would play with his cars, and if he got tired of buzzing, he would tell himself stories and count up to ten, do the alphabet as far as *I,* and if he started to go to sleep he'd pinch himself.

Of course it would have been easier to stay up if there'd been someone to keep him company. He never asked Jim, because Jim wasn't good company. And Franny, if he asked her, always said, "Goodness, what a cute idea" and went to sleep anyway. Well, he would have to do it alone. . . .

"What's that buzzing in there?" Mr. Davis asked his wife. "In the children's room."

"Marshall, of course. Trying to stay up all night."

She was examining Jimmy's winter coat. Mr. Davis was holding a book but not reading it. The rain fell, and after a while the wind rose and whined down the areaway.

Mrs. Davis looked at the coat and pondered. If she let down the hem and the sleeves, wouldn't it do for one more season? Then she wondered why she put it as a question. It would have to do for one more season. One thing, anyway, Jim wouldn't complain. Boys his age didn't much care what they wore so long as no one scolded if they tore it. Franny was another matter. Franny was a girl, and girls wanted —needed—pretty things to wear. Franny had a skirt —too short—a dress, a sweater, and two blouses to see her through the school year. And then their shoes—

She looked up and said, "Do you suppose we could get the children some shoes now that you're working at—"

At the same time, Mr. Davis was saying, "*Why* does he want to stay up all night? What's the reason?"

Since they'd both been talking at once, neither heard what the other had said. Now they fell silent at the same time, started to talk again at the same time, fell silent again. Then carefully Mr. Davis said, "You go first. You say what you were saying, and then I'll say what I was saying."

"It's all right if you say first."

"No, no. I insist. You first."

"Well, then, I said do you think with having the job in the shoe store you could get the children some shoes now?"

"I plan to. As soon as I get established and Mr. Horney, the boss, feels he can't get along without me."

They looked at each other doubtfully. The thought of any boss feeling he couldn't get along without Mr. Davis seemed extreme.

"Still," said Mr. Davis, "you never can tell."

"But just in case he doesn't get to feel that way, couldn't you ask now? I mean, get the shoes now and then sort of work off the price? You should get them wholesale, I think."

"I could try." He paused. "Mr. Horney doesn't exactly have a face that lights up and says 'Love Thy Neighbor.'"

"What does it light up and say?"

" 'Sell More Shoes.' "

Mrs. Davis smiled a little and snipped at the hem of Jim's coat. After a while her husband said, "I'll do it. I'll ask him tomorrow. I made a few sales today. Probably he's already coming to rely on me."

Mr. Davis made no mention of the sale he'd lost because he'd been in the stockroom sketching on a cardboard carton and hadn't even heard the customer come in, call out, wait a while, and go. Mr. Horney had been coming back from lunch just as the customer stormed out angrily through the door. Mr. Horney had taken it badly.

"By Harry," he'd said, "if I had another clerk, I'd throw you out this minute."

On the other hand, Mr. Davis *had* made a few sales during the day, and when Mr. Horney found that the sketch on the cardboard carton was a charcoal drawing of himself, he relented. All the rest of the afternoon he kept glancing at the sketch, and nothing more was said about firing.

Mr. Horney, of course, had no way of knowing that the charcoal portrait was entitled, in Mr. Davis's mind, "Sell More Shoes." Certainly Mr. Davis didn't tell him so. As a result, he wasn't fired, and he now felt confident that he could ask for those shoes tomorrow. I'll finish up the sketch, he told himself. Maybe I'll take it to the studio and touch it up with pastels, give it some color. Then I'll present it to the old boy as a present.

"What were you going to say?" Mrs. Davis asked.

"When?"

"Before. When we were both talking."

"Oh." But Mr. Davis couldn't remember what it had been. By now the buzzing from the other room had ceased, so there was nothing to recall it to him.

Marshall, once again, had failed to stay awake until morning. He hadn't even lasted to midnight, and he never had.

Chapter Four

When Mr. Davis had been sick or when, as had happened since then from time to time, he was out of a job, Franny and Mrs. Davis did the marketing between them, bringing home a little at a time, making it stretch, making it last. But when, as now, he was working, the whole family did the weekly marketing together, making a sort of expedition out of it.

"Men," Mr. Davis said this evening at the door,

"I'm sure you all understand my orders, which I give as captain and commander of this junket. Keep in sight of one another, and *look out for ambushes!*"

"What are ambushes?" Marshall asked.

"They are likely to take the form of something one of you kids wants to buy that we can't afford to buy. There are all sort of ambushes, mind, but that's the chief one we have to be on guard against. So—watch it. Very well. Ready on the right? Ready on the left? Forward *march!*"

As they clattered downstairs Mr. Davis said to Jimmy, "That is a confusion of directions, but the main thing is that everyone understands me. Confusion is nothing, understanding is all."

Jimmy and Franny grinned at their father, and Mrs. Davis laughed. Marshall didn't know what the joke was, but he laughed too because he was happy. He loved marketing nights. Going out at a time when he usually would have been, if not in bed, at least getting ready for it, seemed to him about the best thing that could happen.

The huge, brightly lighted, crowded supermarket down the street had in it about a million things that Marshall coveted and would just about have died to get.

There were potato chips, pickles, jelly fruits, chocolate bars, Eskimo pies, chocolate cookies, soda pop, picture books, games, skipping ropes, drinking mugs with faces on them, little pads of colored paper to write notes on, crayons and paint sets, and cereal boxes that said *Kids! Surprise Inside!!!* Marshall, in spite of knowing the alphabet as far as *I*, couldn't read yet, but he knew those two words.

Surprise Inside!!!

Franny had taught him to read them.

And who could tell what the surprise might be? A tiny red plastic spaceman with tiny helmet and uniform on. A puzzle made of string and cardboard. A tiny book that made a moving picture when you riffled the pages. A balloon with a cat's face on it that grew bigger and bigger as you blew it up. Chinese puzzles, FASCINATING word games. Bird cards, football cards, baseball cards, wild animal cards. One day Franny had read him the back of every sort of cereal box in the store. She had just done FASCINAT-ING WORD GAME when the manager came loping down the aisle and told them to buy or beat it. Marshall had thought that was funny, and he and Franny had laughed as they beat it.

Now as Mr. Davis, wheeling a wire basket before him, took the lead of the expedition, Marshall began to drop back until he was able to slip undetected (they always knew where to find him) to the cereal aisle. Some of the boxes said *Surprise Inside!!!* Some drew a picture on the back of just what you were going to find. Marshall did not know which was more tempting. To know and choose? Or to be surprised?

He was just about to go in search of his mother to remind her that they were out of Grape-Nuts, in case she'd forgotten, when a loud bawling voice arrested his attention.

"But I want it, I want it, I want it!"

A loud and angry boy of about Marshall's age stood beside the shredded wheat, pointing to a plastic drinking glass that had a clown's face on it with eyes that rolled around. *I want that!* he yelled.

"No, dear," said his mother, trying to pull him along. "Not today."

"You get me that, do you hear?" he shouted, pulling away.

"No, Peter," she said. "You can't have it today."

People going by hurried a little, some frowning, some grinning.

"I want it!" Peter screamed. "Get it, I tell you."

His mother walked off toward the soup mixes, her face red. At the end of the aisle she turned and said, "Are you coming or aren't you?"

Marshall waited with interest to see what would happen. There often were children like this in the market. They stamped and yelled until their mamas got tired of listening and let them have the nickel for the bubble gum machine. Or the toy. Or the clown glass. Something. They always seemed to get something.

Suddenly Peter was rolling on the floor, looking very wild and silly. He was gasping and yelling at once, and his mother came running back up the aisle, looking all upset.

"Peter," she said, shaking him. "Oh, my goodness,

what a bad boy you are. *Please* get up off the floor, Peter. If I get you the clown glass, will you promise not to ask for anything else?"

Peter gave a huge sniffle and permitted his mother to pull him off the floor.

"I promise," he said, smiling.

All at once, Marshall decided to try this approach himself. Whenever he asked for anything in the supermarket, Papa always said, "Sorry, Marsh. No," and that was the end of it. He didn't remember that he had ever gotten anything extra just by asking for it, so he decided to try yelling for it.

He hurried to where Mama and Papa, with Franny and Jim, were getting kitchen supplies, cleanser and all. Marshall hadn't decided yet what to yell for, but directly across the aisle were the picture books, with lambs and kittens and puppies in colors on the covers. He decided to want one of those.

Planting himself squarely in front of them, he said loudly, "I want a picture book. I want that one with the bunny on it."

Mrs. Davis didn't pay any attention. She was comparing the difference between two different kinds of detergent, telling Franny how she should check not only the price but the amount of detergent the box contained. Franny listened, absorbed, and Jimmy was half listening to them, half looking at Marshall, in a superior way.

"There, now," said Mr. Davis to Jimmy. "Didn't I

46 ✳

tell you? Your brother has fallen into an ambush. We must form a rescue party. There isn't a minute to lose."

"We'll pull him out," said Jimmy, moving forward with a grin. "We'll drag him out of the ambush by his ears!"

But Marshall, in a sudden rush of greed, had lost track of the family game. He didn't care now about ambushes or rescue parties. He just wanted a picture book with a bunny on the cover.

"I tell you I want it!" he yelled.

All at once Mr. Davis dropped his role of captain and commander of the expedition. He became a father. "Nope," said this father. "Sorry, but no money."

"I don't care, I don't care," Marshall said, stamping his foot. "You get me that, do you hear?"

By now Mama, Papa, Franny, and Jim were all staring at him. The fun had gone out of the shopping expedition, and they were just looking at him.

"I don't know what's gotten into you," said Mr. Davis, "but the answer is *N-O*. No. Now stop behaving this way."

Marshall felt his heart sink, but he was too far in to back out now. He stood, legs apart, eyes narrowed, and began to hold his breath. He held it until he frightened everybody, even himself. He could feel his heart knocking and his eyes popping, but he went on holding it until, far away and sort of fuzzily, he heard his mother say, "Marshall, you stop that. You'll hurt yourself."

"Well, I'm not going to stay and watch this," Jim said, walking quickly away. Marshall sensed rather than heard him leave, because by this time his ears were ringing and he couldn't see. And still he held his breath.

"Oh, dear," he heard his mother cry out, "what are we going to do?"

"We aren't going to do anything," Mr. Davis said loudly. "We are going to wait and do nothing, and in a second Marshall will start breathing again because there's nothing else he can do."

Indeed, at that moment the breath rushed from Marshall's lungs, leaving him weak and shaky. "You're mean, mean," he sobbed. "You're an awful, horrible papa."

"And you're a dreadful little boy," Franny said.

Marshall gulped and stared at his sister in despair. Franny! Franny had said he was a dreadful little boy. "I'm not," he protested miserably. "I am not so."

"Yes. A silly bad baby, that's what you are."

"No!"

"Yes. When Papa says there's no money for something, he means there is *no* money. You should be ashamed, acting this way."

"But he always says there's no money," Marshall wailed.

"That's because there never is any," Mr. Davis said crossly. "Now if you've finished behaving like an idiot, we'll get on with the marketing."

Marshall scowled, sniffled, stumped along behind them, past the dairy department, the meat department, the household products department, and finally past the checker and so out into the street, where by now it was beginning to get dark. When they got to the sidewalk, Marshall saw Peter and his mother going down the street. Peter was holding his clown glass and skipping happily. Marshall looked after him for a moment and then followed his own family.

The streetlamps were on now and the sidewalks thronged with people. Music came out of open windows, since it was a warm September night, and the screened doors of restaurants and delicatessens allowed you to see the people inside, eating or pointing to salamis or getting pickles out of little barrels.

The Davises marched along, Papa carrying a heavy bag, Mama, Jimmy, and Franny a smaller bag each, and Marshall nothing at all. He trailed them a little, not enough to get lost but enough to show them that he was still displeased. He was gratified to see that both his mother and Franny took quick looks over their shoulders to be sure of him.

They sauntered along. Later in the year, when it was raining or grew cold, they would hurry with heads bent, wanting to get to the warmth and dryness of their apartment as quickly as possible. But now in the early autumn there was no need for haste. They stopped and looked in different shops. A Mexican store with silver and blue jewelry lying on woven rugs. A store with baskets of fruit all wrapped and ribboned. A Chinese laundry, from which came a hot clean smell that Marshall found wonderful.

There were lots of people and animals. Dogs on leashes, dogs running free, cats in doorways smoothing their whiskers. There were children younger than Marshall himself, running as free, it seemed, as the dogs. Anyway nobody yelled for them to come here, or come upstairs, or didn't they know it was bedtime? They seemed to go about just as they wanted. Marshall wondered if he would like to be able to do that, decided that on the whole he wouldn't. To be out on the street in the dark with Papa and Mama was fine and fun. But he guessed he wouldn't like it so much without them.

Suddenly he hurried to catch up with his family, because they had stopped at a pushcart, and this was the part of marketing that Marshall liked best of all. There were lots of pushcarts on the street, but usually Mama stopped at Pepi's.

"Does Pepi have the best produce?" Papa had asked once, and Mama had said, "No, but he has the nicest moustache."

Pepi's moustache was pretty grand. It was very thick and went out to the sides for a couple of inches and then up for a couple more. Now as the Davises came up to him he tipped his old hat and said, *"Buona sera, buona sera,* how is my favorite family this evening?"

Mama said he said that to everybody, but it sounded so real that she and Franny had decided every family really was his favorite. "Whichever one he's seeing is his favorite one to see," Mama had decided. "What a nice way to be."

"Buona sera, Pepi," said the Davises, and the careful business of buying fruits and vegetables began.

Pepi's cart was piled high with apples, red and yellow, with huge black grapes dappled silver, with green and orange squashes shaped like barrels, and clusters of gold bananas hanging from a pole across the top. At the end of the cart was a round basket full of bronze and lavender chrysanthemums. Mrs. Davis gave them one longing glance and then looked away. Sometimes they bought flowers, but this was not to be one of the times.

Tonight, arranged in long frail wooden cartons, were bunches of dark purple Concord grapes, those grapes that come only in autumn. When they are eaten cold the sweet-sour globe inside the dark skin bursts against the teeth and sends juices like wine trickling down the throat. The very sight of them made Marshall's mouth water.

"Mama," he said, pulling at her sleeve, "get some of those, please?"

She smiled down at him. "Since you ask so nicely, Marshall . . . all right."

So they bought a little bunch of those and two barrel squashes and five bananas. Marshall carried that bag himself.

As they walked away Mr. Davis said, "I do believe sometimes that Pepi's pushcart is one of the most beautiful sights in this city. What do you say, Franny?"

"Except maybe for Pepi's moustache," she said, and they laughed.

The bells of St. Anthony of Padua rang out. One

. . . two . . . three . . . Marshall counted, lost count, smiled, and no one looking at him could have believed that he was a boy who had just recently stamped his feet and yelled and held his breath in the aisle of a supermarket, all over a picture book that he hadn't really wanted anyway.

Chapter Five

Although Marshall tried to be as good as he knew how with Mrs. Mundy, she scolded quite a bit. For instance now. They were on their way to the market to do Mrs. Mundy's grocery shopping, and Mrs. Mundy was in a hurry. She was always in a hurry, and she always said, "Hurry now, Marshall, we'll be late." She said it now again.

"Hurry, Marshall. We'll be late."

"For what?" he asked, dragging back a bit. She

was holding his hand and pulling him along so fast he was almost running.

"Don't be sassy."

Marshall dug in his heels and they both stopped in the middle of the sidewalk. "I've got a pain in my side," he said.

"Oh, my goodness." She leaned over him. "What sort of pain?"

"It's a stitch from going too fast. That's what Franny says."

"What Franny says when?"

"When I tell her how I get this pain in my side from running to the market."

Mrs. Mundy set her lips. "Tch, tch," she said. "I'm surprised at you, Marshall. A tattletale. That's what you turned out to be."

"Not true," said Marshall indignantly. "Not true. We were just talking about how people get pains. Like in the winter, in the wind, my ears hurt. Franny says hers do too. And so then I told her how I get this pain when I run, and she says it's a stitch. She gets them when they have recess at school and do races and things."

They were walking again but not so fast. "Do you ever get pains, Mrs. Mundy?" Marshall asked. He was scrunching his hand around in hers, trying to get loose. But the more he scrunched, the more she held on. It really was awful. As if he was a baby or would run away if she didn't hang on to him. Marshall wondered whether he *would* run away if she let go. He realized he would not. He'd be scared of getting lost.

"Yes, I do," said Mrs. Mundy.

"What do you?" he asked, having forgotten his question.

"I do get pains," she informed him severely.

"From running?" he asked.

"From boys."

"Oh." Marshall thought for a while. "But I'm the only boy that's around you," he pointed out. Mrs. Mundy's own children were all grown up and had been a disappointment to her. He knew that because she'd told him.

"Exactly," she said, and grabbed his hand tighter because they were about to cross a street. All of a sudden she stopped, hugged him close. "Excuse me, Marshall," she said. "That was not a nice thing for me to say."

"No, it wasn't," he agreed.

Still, when she hugged him he didn't mind if she'd been cross. She had this way of being cross and then nice. Marshall had discovered that most grown-up people were like that. In fact, of all the people in the world, the only one who was always nice was Franny. His mother and father were nice most of the time. Jim was awful most of the time. Mrs. Mundy was nice some of the time and awful some of the time. But Franny was always the same. Even when he'd held his breath in the supermarket and Franny had said he was a bad boy, still Marshall knew she hadn't changed.

By now he and Mrs. Mundy had arrived at the same market, and Marshall was released to tag along after her tall thin form as she pushed her wire wagon from the vegetables to the canned goods to the soaps to the dairy.

"We need some cornflakes," he said as they passed the cereals. There was a tiger on the back of the cornflakes box, and Marshall knew, because he had a lion, that inside was a cardboard cutout that would make a little animal if you put it together right. "We need them awful bad."

"But I don't," said Mrs. Mundy.

"But we do. Mama said."

"Then your mama will buy some."

"She might forget."

"Marshall, my job is to look after you, not to do your marketing."

"But—"

"No buts. Besides, I have only enough money to do my own buying, and not much of that."

Marshall subsided. *Not enough money.* There was no way to answer that. Unless he wanted to try holding his breath again. He had a feeling that it would work out no better with Mrs. Mundy than it had with Papa and Mama. Besides—besides he didn't want to, not ever again. Not for a cardboard tiger or a clown glass or anything. He lingered, looking over the other boxes, and when he looked up Mrs. Mundy had disappeared. Marshall, unalarmed, started off in search of her just as she came striding back, pushing her wagon furiously and looking from side to side.

"There you are," she said. "Where did you go?"

"I didn't go anywhere," Marshall pointed out. "I stayed here. You went to—"

She didn't let him finish. "Oh, what a bad boy you are," she said. "What a bad boy."

"No, I'm not," Marshall said calmly. "I'm a very good boy."

When they got home, Marshall helped Mrs. Mundy to put away her groceries, and then it was three o'clock, so he went out in the hall to wait for Franny.

"What shall we do?" she asked, as she always did. "Play first or work first?"

Marshall, as he always did, said, "Play."

"All right. What shall we play?"

"School."

That too was what he always said first. Sometimes they played different things afterward.

"Do you want to be teacher, or shall I?"

Marshall hesitated. He loved being teacher, standing up while Franny sat on the little chair. Still, they never did seem to learn as much when he was teacher, and Marshall was in a hurry to learn everything. Partly to catch up with Jim. Partly because he just liked learning things.

"You be," he said. "I think I'd like to learn *X* today."

"Marshall, you can't learn *X* yet. You have to learn —oh, a *lot* of letters before you get to *X*."

"Can't we skip?" he complained. "I *want* to learn *X*."

"No. You'd get all mixed up."

"I wouldn't either."

"Then I would. The alphabet goes in order, Marshall, and you have to go in order after it. That's one of the nice things about arithmetic and the alphabet. If you stopped thinking about them for a hundred years, at the end of it two and two would still be four and *J* would still come before *K*. They're even better than geography that way."

"What does geography do?"

"It changes all the time," Franny complained.

"Then why do you like it best?"

"Why do you like chocolate better than vanilla?" she asked.

Marshall saw that there were some things that couldn't be answered.

"Now, pupil," said Franny, "if you will take your seat, we will get started on our lessons. Today we shall learn the letter *J*."

Marshall sat happily in the little chair, picked up the pencil, and held it ready.

"*J*," he repeated. Franny formed the letter on her pad of paper, and he copied it on his. "What does *J* stand for, teacher?"

"Well, let me see. *J* stands for joy and jump and and jelly bean—"

"And jelly roll and jellyfish and jelly crullers and jelly doughnuts and—"

The teacher held up her hand. "Very good," she said. "You have caught on nicely. But *J* doesn't just stand for jelly things. It also stands for jungle and juice and jacks and jitters. It stands for Jim too."

"It does?" Marshall wrinkled his nose, put down his pencil. "I guess I won't learn *J.*"

"Don't be silly," said Franny, sounding a little like their mother or father. "You can't not learn a letter just because Jim's name starts with it. He has to start his name with some letter, doesn't he?"

"But I don't want to learn his letter," Marshall said stubbornly. "He knocked me down."

"Oh, Marsh. He did not," Franny said, laughing. "Or if he did it was partly your own fault. Now do you or don't you want to go on with the lesson?"

"Let's not do the alphabet today," Marshall decided. "Let's do history."

"All right. Who was George Washington?"

"The first president."

"Of what?"

Marshall looked blank, so Franny said, "President of what, Marsh? There are presidents of all sorts of things. Banks, colleges, student bodies, committees. What was George Washington president of?"

"People?" Marshall guessed uncertainly.

"Well . . . that's sort of an answer. George Washington was the first president of the United States."

"Yes," Marshall agreed.

Franny sat down on the sofa, indicating that school was over for the day.

"Let's play the one where we say what we're going to be when we grow up," she said. "What do you want to be, Marshall? President?"

"Of what?"

"Of anything."

"Could I be president of a zoo?"

Franny didn't think he could.

Marshall shook his head. "I guess I won't be a president," he said.

"That's all right," she assured him. "Do you know what I want to be? Now promise not to laugh." Marshall promised. "Well," Franny said slowly, "I want to be a mermaid."

Marshall's eyes widened. "But, Franny," he protested. "You can't swim."

"I know," she said dreamily. "But if I were a mermaid, I wouldn't have to learn, I'd just know. Oh, it would be beautiful. I'd loll on the warm ocean and comb my hair and sing and marry a merprince. I would not," she added, caught up in this fancy, "fall in love with a human prince and lose my voice and turn into foam."

Marshall was liking this less and less. "I don't think you can grow up to be a mermaid, Franny. I think you have to start out being one."

"Oh, I know," she said, smiling. "I was only fooling. But it would be fun, wouldn't it, Marsh?"

"I don't think so. I'd be afraid of drowning."

"Well, if I can't be a mermaid, I'll be a toe dancer."

"That would be nice."

"Of course," she added, looking downcast, "you have to start being a dancer practically as early as a mermaid. You have to take lessons for years and years."

"But you dance very nice. Like a bird on the wing—" he began, and waited. But Franny just kept on looking sad, so he finished for her, "you dance and you sing. Remember, Franny?"

"Oh . . . that's just talk. Any girl who really wants to be a dancer *has* to have lessons. Lila Wembleton takes dancing lessons, and the way she talks, my goodness, you'd think she was queen of the May."

Marshall, who did not in the least like hearing his sunny sister go on in this gloomy manner, said, "I'll tell Papa you want to be a toe dancer, and I bet he'll get you some lessons."

Franny sighed and shook her head. "Don't say anything to him, Marshall. We don't have money for things like that."

"Why?"

"Why what?"

"Why don't we have any money, ever, for things?"

"Oh, my goodness, Marshall. Because, that's all. Just because."

"I've decided what I want to be when I grow up," Marshall said.

Franny smiled at him. "What, darling?"

"Rich."

"Well, that's a good idea, I suppose," Franny said doubtfully. In the stories she read, people who wished to be rich always ended up back in the hovel, worse off than they'd been to start with. It was like getting the three wishes. You knew right away when someone in a story got offered three wishes, he'd be smart to turn down the whole idea at the beginning. And yet you couldn't help thinking how if *you* had been offered three wishes, how *you* would be so careful and smart—

"And I'll stay up all night, every night." Marshall was going on with his plans for being grown up. "If Mama and Papa will let me," he added.

"*Why* do you want to stay up all night?" she asked.

Marshall shrugged. "Because."

Since *because* always seemed to them a pretty reasonable reason, they accepted it, and presently lost interest in the future.

"I know," Marshall said, brightening. "Now I'll tell you what I want for my birthday."

Franny jumped to her feet. "You get out the silverware, Marshall, and start setting the table. If you're very good, I'll let you scrub the potatoes.

Would you like that?" When he didn't move, she burst into song: "Oh, potatoes and tomatoes, boom, bam, bom. If your name wasn't Marshall, it might be Tom!"

Marshall, who had been trying to glare and be angry because she wouldn't pay attention to his birthday wishes, started to smile and then to laugh.

"Bam, bom, boom!" he yelled. "If my name wasn't Marshall, it might be . . . SKLOOM!"

"Bom, boom, bam. If my name was Mathilda, then it wouldn't be Fran!"

"Oh, potatoes and tomatoes . . . fie, fo, fum—"

"If you two weren't so silly, you'd just be dumb!"

There was Jim, half scowling, half smiling, in the doorway. It was the first time he'd ever joined in the game, and it made them both laugh more than ever.

Chapter Six

Franny and Simone were working on their scrapbooks together. They had a pile of magazines, some scissors, paste, and several hours of Friday afternoon ahead of them. Mr. Orgella was at work, Mrs. Orgella had gone to see a neighbor, Grandmother Orgella was napping in the bedroom. Marshall, with some of the other Orgella children, had gone to the park with Francisco, their cousin from San Juan. That left Simone and Franny with only the baby to take care of. He was asleep now, but so darling that Franny would gladly have given up her scrapbook pasting in order to play with him.

Simone cut from the magazines pictures of beautiful rooms, beautiful people, beautiful flowers, and once in a while an animal if it was presented in an especially beautiful way. She'd found a picture of a black cat wearing a ruby necklace, and though Franny had already just about decided to take it, Simone got in there first with "That's mine."

Franny sighed. Whoever said "that's mine" first got the picture, but she wished she'd yelled first. She just hadn't expected Simone to take a cat. Usually Simone wanted pictures of absolutely gorgeous bathrooms with lavender towels and purple rugs and goldfish for faucets. Or people in evening clothes looking at New York City from a penthouse at night. Or bottles of perfume growing out of bouquets of roses. Or people on golf courses smiling at their cigarette coupons. That was the sort of thing Simone liked. Franny tended to cut animal pictures and pictures of other lands and any map she could find, and advertisements that had nothing but colored shapes on them. Simone had a lot of black-and-white pictures in her scrapbook. Franny didn't even have one.

They snipped and pasted happily. The sound of scissors cutting through glossy paper, the sharp spicy

odor of paste, the delicate business of fitting a new picture onto a page so that it went well with what was there—all this was absorbing, and sometimes minutes went by during which they didn't speak.

Simone carefully affixed a woman in a fur wrap, which she had neatly cut out around the figure and not just square around the advertisement.

"There," she said. "That's nice."

Franny looked. "What sort of fur is that?"

"Oh, Franny. It's chinchilla. The precious fur for the precious few." When Franny looked blank, Simone pointed to the magazine. "That's what it says there. The precious fur for the precious few."

"What does it mean?"

"You have to be rich to get it."

"You mean you have to be precious."

"Same thing, I guess," Said Simone. "Anyway you can see that not many people have it. I will someday."

Simone often predicted what she would have someday. It was usually something expensive. Still, she nearly always added, as she did now, "I'll get one for Mama too. And Consuelo. And you too, Franny."

"Where are you going to get the money?"

"I'll—I guess I'll be an actress," Simone said thoughtfully. "They make acres of money, and everybody's crazy about them and they travel everywhere. And they wear these beautiful clothes all the time."

"There's a girl in our building who's an actress. All she ever wears is black pants and a sweater and sandals. Her feet are always dirty."

"Maybe she's a dancer. They get their feet dirty from stamping around barefoot. A modern dancer," Simone explained, because Franny didn't always understand these things.

"I'd like to be a toe dancer," Franny said. Her eyes grew dreamy and she saw herself spinning across a stage . . . fluffy skirt, white satin shoes, a diamond crown on her head, and music playing to her steps.

"Ballet," Simone corrected. "Ballet dancer. You don't say toe dancer, Franny."

Simone knew things like that. Franny figured it was because the Orgellas had a television set. The Davises hadn't. Mr. Davis said it was one of the minor blessings of poverty, but Franny and Jim and Marshall didn't think it was a blessing.

"All right," she said agreeably. "Ballet dancer. But I would. Like to be one."

"Lila Wembleton takes ballet lessons."

"Well, she's rich, too," Franny said, abandoning her dream. She wasn't sure she wanted to share a career with Lila. "Except Papa says maybe she isn't. Owning your own building in these parts doesn't mean you're rich, necessarily, Papa says."

They considered this.

"She doesn't have a lunch pass," Franny said. "And she takes toe-dancing lessons. I guess she's rich. Are you still mad at her?'' Franny hoped this was the case but could hardly say so.

Simone lifted her shoulders. "She's best friends with Ginny now, anyway, so what's the diff? The thing about her and Ginny is, they're both only children. I mean they don't have any brothers or sisters. If you're an only child, you have lots of time to be together with somebody instead of always having to take care of—''

José took that moment to cry out, and Simone rushed to the basket where he lay. "Aren't I awful?'' she said to him softly. "But you know I didn't really mean it.'' She leaned over and patted him on the stomach, and in a moment he was asleep again. "You'd think he heard me,'' she said, coming back to sit at the table with Franny.

"I wouldn't like it at all,'' Franny said firmly. "Being an only child. I wouldn't even give up Jimmy, and he's a terrible pest most of the time.''

"Only, maybe, just not so many,'' Simone said, staring around. "I wouldn't give anybody *up*, you know. But it just gets so crowded.''

The Orgella apartment was about as crowded as a place could be and still permit the people to move around from place to place. The living room, where they were now, had a flowery rug so big it had to be folded where it met the wall. Mr. Orgella was in the housewrecking business, and somebody whose house he'd wrecked had given it to him. All the Orgellas were pleased with it, as before it came they'd had just the wooden floor with no covering. The rug muffled sounds, made everything warmer, made it nicer for the little children to play on the floor, and lent, generally, a nice fancy touch to the room. There were other fancy things: plant holders shaped like shoes; lots of photographs of the family—here and in San Juan—in frames on the tables and the upright piano; bright chintz curtains that were really made of paper only you practically had to feel them to know it; and a little shelf on the wall with a Madonna on it. She wore a blue robe and had a red glass cup at her feet. There was usually a candle burning in it, and Franny thought it was lovely.

There were things to sleep on everywhere. The grandmother slept in one bedroom with all the girls, two of them in bed with her and Simone on a cot. In the other bedroom the boys slept, and now that Francisco was with them the two smaller ones had to sleep in one cot with their feet in each other's faces. They thought it was pretty funny. Like Franny's own parents, the Orgellas had a folding couch in the living room.

"Lila Wembleton has her own room all to herself," Simone said now. "I've been there lots. She has toy stuffed animals all over her bed and a dressing table with a pink skirt and a little phonograph all her own. Franny, stop *doing* that."

"Doing what?"

"Picking at that—that scab"— Simone winced at the word—"on your knee."

Franny, not even noticing, had been gently trying to peel away a scab that had formed on her knee from the last time she'd fallen down rollerskating. Her knees were always in the process of healing, always being freshly damaged. She looked at Simone's knees, smooth as satin, without even smudges on them. And Simone was as good a rollerskater as she was.

"Well, it's just too bad about you, Simone," she said. "I guess I can pick at my—my knees if I want to without getting bossed around by you."

"Oh, of course you can," Simone said lightly. "Go right ahead. I'm only telling you, because I'm your friend, how ugly it looks, picking that way. That's all. I'm just telling you."

"Well, I'm just telling you that I'm sick and tired of hearing about rich Lila Wembleton and her room to herself and her no brothers and sisters, see? I'm just *telling* you, that's all."

"All right," said Simone. "You've told me."

They worked on their scrapbooks in silence now and were glad when the baby woke up and began to cry, giving them a chance to start talking again. They found José so marvelous that they forgot to be angry with each other.

"Don't you just adore the way his mouth turns down when he cries?" Franny said. "Look at how cute he is."

72 ✖

José waved his arms and legs and let the tears fall from his dark and beautiful eyes.

"You can hold him, Franny," Simone said, "while I heat his bottle."

Franny, who would have liked to lift José from the basket, didn't quite dare. She waited while Simone, competent as a nurse, lifted the howling baby, changed his diaper, held him against her shoulder for a moment, then handed him over to Franny as if he were no more breakable than a rubber ball. Franny sat on the sofa, full of pride and love because José, in her arms, quieted down and began to look about alertly, kicking his legs and clutching at her finger.

Simone was heating the bottle. She didn't have to leave the room because the kitchen was against the wall, with just a screen that could be dropped down to hide it when not in use. The Orgellas didn't bother to drop the screen at all, and Franny thought that was awful. If it had been hers, she'd have hidden the wall kitchen from view whenever she could.

Franny, who could understand geography, arithmetic, and some pretty complicated books, had difficulty understanding people. She could not see, for instance, why a girl like Simone, who loved pretty things so much, never seemed to care what her home looked like. Simone just dropped things wherever she was and had to be forced to help with the housecleaning. Franny couldn't see why Jimmy, who was a smart enough boy, was always doing things that any

73 ❄

dumbbell could tell would get him into trouble. And maybe most of all, she could not understand why her father, the nicest, smartest, dearest man in the world, kept losing jobs, so that she and Jimmy had to have lunch passes and never have any new clothes, and Mama had to work all the time instead of staying home the way lots of mothers did.

Well, there didn't seem to be any answer except to wait and hope that one day she'd learn to understand things like this. She didn't want to ask Simone why she didn't let the curtain down in front of the kitchen now that the formula was heated. She couldn't ask her father why he shouldn't try harder this time and maybe keep his job. She held José close and listened to his gurgles and his little sudden sighs and sighed herself without realizing it.

"Francisco doesn't like it here," Simone said. She was putting away the magazines and scissors and paste. "Are you going to leave your scrapbook here or take it home?"

Franny hesitated. Sometimes she left it here, almost like a guarantee that she'd have an excuse to come back even if she and Simone had another of their quarrels. She was all at once angry with herself for this. Simone never left anything at *her* house for a guarantee. That was another thing that confused Franny. Why were some people so sure of themselves, while other people, in spite of straight *A*'s, were always wondering if they'd made a mistake or were just about to make one? Sometimes Franny thought she'd have to wait to be grown up before she really understood anything.

"I'm going to take it home," she said loudly. "I want to show Marshall the new pictures. Why doesn't Francisco like it here?"

"He says it's cold."

"But it isn't cold yet at all. It's lovely weather."

Simone rolled up her dark eyes, put her hand to her chest. "Here," she said. "In the heart. Francisco says New York has a cold heart."

"Oh. Well, he hasn't been here very long."

"No."

"Who's coldhearted? You—I mean your family isn't coldhearted."

"Francisco doesn't mean us."

"Who does he mean?" Franny asked, lifting José to her shoulder. His head bobbed, fell against her neck, lifted again. He gave a big happy burp. Franny put her hand up to steady him, loving the warm round way the back of his head just fitted into her open palm. Darling little José. She wished she could remember Marshall at this age, but she couldn't, not really. She'd been only about six or so herself when he was born.

"He means"—Simone threw her arms wide—"the world up here. The whole world."

For a moment Franny forgot what they were talking about and then remembered Francisco. "But what's wrong? What happened to make him feel that way?"

"He can't get a job."

"Oh." Franny couldn't think of anything to add. Her own father had so much difficulty with jobs that she certainly knew the complaint. What she didn't know was anything to say about it. *Why not?* seemed a pretty silly question. Still, after a moment's silence she said, "Why not?"

"Francisco says it's because he's a foreigner."

"But he isn't," Franny said sharply. She was always annoyed when Simone knew less than she did herself and never remembered the times when Simone knew more. "A person from Puerto Rico is as much an American as a person from Brooklyn."

"Maybe so," said Simone in a disbelieving tone.

"There's no maybe about it," said Franny, the geography expert.

"What *you* say is so, Franny Davis, and what happens to people isn't always the same thing. And if Francisco feels like a foreigner here, that's how people have made him feel."

"Maybe he makes himself feel that way."

Simone, looking baffled, decided to change the subject. "Let's make some popcorn," she said. "Francisco bought us an electric corn popper. Mama says if he keeps on this way he won't have money to get back to San Juan, if he decides to go back. I personally would go back in a flash."

"You can't go back. You've never been there."

"I'd go back, even so," Simone said stubbornly. "I would adore to live in San Juan."

"But what about all your family? I mean, would you just go off and leave everybody and live in San Juan by yourself?" Would you just go off and leave me? she thought. But she didn't say it.

"I wouldn't be by myself if Francisco went back. Besides we've got lots of family down there. No, I wouldn't be alone at all."

"But your mama and papa. And José. What about them?" What about me? Still she didn't say it.

"Oh, well," Simone said a bit crossly. "What difference does it make since I can't go anyway? I have to stay up here where it's sleety and slushy for months and the sun doesn't shine for weeks at a time and everything is gray and cold—"

"Oh, Simone. You sound as if we lived in Alaska."

"I feel as if I lived in Alaska."

"Simone, that's so silly. Alaska is in an entirely different temperature zone than we are. Alaska is in—"

"Well, I guess I'm not the only silly one in the world," Simone interrupted. "I just guess not. And I don't go around picking and pulling at my *scabs* all the time."

They glared at each other.

"Here, let me have José," said Simone.

Franny handed him over, and Simone put him

77 ✳

back in the basket, where he gave a brief protesting wail and fell asleep. Then Grandmother Orgella came into the room, yawning and shuffling her slippers. In another moment pounding feet and voices on the stairs announced the homecoming of Francisco with the children.

When they all erupted into the room it was like a schoolyard at recess, with everybody talking and shouting at once. The noise woke José, who began to cry, which made Grandmother Orgella angry. She lifted her thin sharp voice, berating everyone, but nobody listened until Francisco, with a bellow that rose above the din, told everybody to shut up or he'd tie them all together with Scotch tape and fasten them to the wall. This sent the children into gales of laughter and even Grandmother Orgella, who was usually cross, giggled a little.

"Okay, then," said Francisco when some order had been restored. His eye fell on the corn popper. "Okay then. We'll all pop corn and I'll sing for you."

So for a while they sat quietly listening to Francisco as he played on his gaudy guitar and sang in his deep voice about a dark-haired lady who never could be tried or true, while the corn popped and pinged against the aluminum lid of the new electric popper.

Later, when Franny with her scrapbook and her brother was down in the street on the way home, she remembered that she and Simone had not made up this time. Of course they would because they always did. She was sure of that. Only maybe even quite good friends could quarrel once too often. Anyway it hadn't been nice of Simone, not nice at all, to talk that way. I mean, Franny said to herself, I wouldn't tell her that something she did was ugly, no matter what it was.

"Francisco sings good," said Marshall.

"Sings well," Franny corrected.

Marshall accepted that patiently. "I liked the one about the bee in the rain forest, didn't you?"

"Yes."

"I guess a rain forest is a forest where it rains all the time."

"I guess it is."

Finding that Franny wasn't in a talking mood, Marshall began to hum to himself as he trudged along with the scrapbook in his arms.

That evening Franny said to her father, "Is it harder to get a job in America if you're a foreigner? I mean, even if you aren't one, like from Puerto Rico, but you feel like one?"

"I don't think I'm the ideal job consultant," he said, trying to laugh the question away. But when Franny continued to look at him, waiting for the serious, sensible reply she knew she could get if she waited long enough, he sighed a bit, put his newspaper down, and said, "Yes. I'm afraid under most circumstances it is."

"Why?"

"Oh, Franny. Oh, Franny." He stared around the room. "I can't give you an answer, just like that. It's how things are."

"But it isn't fair, is it?"

"No."

"Then why did it turn out that way?"

Mr. Davis rubbed his cheek with his hand, then the back of his neck. Then he looked at his wife, but she just looked back at him, and by this time Jim too was waiting to see what he'd say. Even Marshall, who hadn't heard the question, was waiting for the answer.

"For reasons," Mr. Davis said at last, "that are too long and complicated to go into, this seems to be the way of mankind. Whoever got there first is superior."

"Got where?" said Jim.

"Anywhere. If my family has been in America a hundred years and yours has been here ten years, then I'm better than you are. That's the way people figure. But don't ask me to explain that; it's too preposterous for explanations. It's the same in all countries."

"What about the American Indian?" said Jim. "He was in this country first, and look what happened to him. I bet the American Indian doesn't feel superior."

"Ah, but you're overlooking another human truth," said Mr. Davis. "Conquerors are best of all.

And that," he said, forestalling Franny's response, "isn't fair either. But you find as you get older that life does not usually undertake to be fair or logical. Please don't ask me to explain that."

"It's like me," Mrs. Davis said suddenly. As always when she spoke, everyone turned to listen. Franny had decided that this was because her mother talked so little that people just naturally wanted to hear what she said when she did say something.

"Like you how?" Jimmy asked her encouragingly, since she'd fallen silent again.

"I feel," she began slowly, "as if—as if there were so many things I might have done, might have understood, except that I didn't get a chance in time to understand them. When I came from Ireland fifteen years ago, I was what you call an unskilled worker. And that's what I still am."

"Why?" said Franny. Jimmy scowled at her and she scowled back. "I'm not saying anything bad. I only want to *know*."

"Of course you want to know," Mrs. Davis said, sighing. "But do I know? Yes, perhaps I do. Because I—" She stopped.

"Because," said Mr. Davis, "she met me, and we got married and along came you children, and then I got sick, and, and, *and*—so it has gone, so it always goes. There is never enough time. No time to learn a skill, no time to understand all those things that take time in the understanding."

"What sort of things?" Jimmy asked, looking at his mother.

"Oh—" She smiled at them. "Well, take the stars. I look at the stars sometimes and I think to myself, I *could* have been an astronomer. Yes, really. I would like to understand about the stars. I *could* understand about the stars, but I'd have to have learned so much else first. And the fact is, I only finished what is grammar school in this country. So—the stars for me are only to look at."

She'd had a faraway look in her eyes as she spoke, and now all at once she seemed to return to this room and these listeners, and she laughed.

"Nobody must get confused by this, you know. I wouldn't trade what I have for a skyful of stars. All of you—you're what I want. It's just that . . ." She turned out her hands helplessly.

"You'd just like to have both," Jimmy said.

"Yes," she answered softly. "It would have been good to have both. Still in all, you three will go to school and maybe even to college, and maybe one day we will have an astronomer in the family." She stood up, patting Marshall on the head. "And now I must clear the table."

When she'd gone to the kitchen, Mr. Davis picked up his newspaper, held it a moment, let it fall to the floor. To distract him, Franny said, "Papa, do you think you could get Francisco a job at your shoe store? He can't get a job, and he says everybody up here has a cold heart, and so I thought—"

"*My* shoe store," Mr. Davis said with a snort. "She calls it my shoe store. Look, Franny, I've got enough trouble hanging onto a job myself. I bet the president of the United States couldn't get a job in that shoe store if I recommended him to Mr. Horney. Mr. Horney would probably say, 'I'm sorry, Mr. President, but your references just aren't good enough,' and the president would have to go away and try to get a job someplace else."

"He's already got one," Jim pointed out.

"Well, it's a good thing he isn't relying on me," said Mr. Davis.

Franny realized there was no use pleading Francisco's case anymore. She decided to stop thinking about the Orgellas because it made her sad to think of Francisco and annoyed to think of Simone. And she didn't want to think about her mother and the stars because that bewildered her.

"Come on, Marsh," she said. "Do you want to look at my scrapbook now? I got a lot of new animals today and some pictures of the back of the moon."

Marshall, who'd never thought about the back of the moon before, now realized there was nothing he'd rather see. They settled down on the floor together as Jim went grumbling to the kitchen to help his mother with the dishes.

Chapter Seven

It was Saturday morning. Hank Washington, Nick Straus, and Jim Davis met by arrangement on the street corner. Each carried a shopping bag of heavy brown paper, and they set off without a word to the nearest apartment building. When they got inside they climbed to the top floor, went to a door, and rang the bell. Nick and Hank stood slightly behind Jim.

The door opened and Jim looked up at the woman

who stood there. He smiled. His smile was very like his father's, so that the woman, who'd been about to close her door again at the sight of three ragged rather tough-looking boys, hesitated and said, "Is there something I can do for you?"

"What it is, lady," said Jim, "is do you have any old deposit bottles that we could help you out by taking away? They get piled up and get to be sort of a nuisance around the apartment and what we do is we take them—"

"And get the deposit," she said sharply.

Jim nodded. "We're collecting for this fund, like. For poor children. Everything we get goes to them."

The woman softened. "Well, now, isn't that good of you boys. You give up a beautiful morning like this to do charitable work?"

"Yes, ma'am," said Jim. His manners in these interviews were so remarkable that Hank and Nick had a hard time keeping their faces straight. "That's right, ma'am."

"I guess I have some," she said, stepping back. "You just wait out here and I'll bring them to you."

"Boy," said Nick, when the door had closed. "Boy. First crack out of the box."

"And she didn't even ask what fund," Hank marveled. "Some people are awful dumb."

"Shut up," said Jim. "She's coming."

They got four big bottles and six small ones, and, as Nick had pointed out, it was the first crack out of the box. However, their luck immediately took a turn for the worse. A lot of doors didn't open at all, and of those that did, most slammed immediately in their faces. One man looked at them sourly when Jim mentioned the fund and said he just bet they gave the money to poor kids, he just bet they did.

Going out of that building and down the street to the next, Hank said, "What a crumb, what a toad. You'd think we were lying or something."

They burst out laughing, and then Jim said, "Well, it's not so bad. We got thirty-two cents worth. Let's keep going till we get up to seventy-five. Then we'll have a quarter each to spend."

"May take us all day," Hank grumbled.

Jim shrugged. "Let's go."

By ten o'clock they hadn't collected another bottle.

"The heck with it," Nick said. "Let's cash in these. What's three into thirty-two?"

"Almost eleven cents each," Jim said.

"What do you mean, almost?"

Jim looked pained. "What do you mean, what do I mean, almost? It's this word means *almost*, see? Now, if we could get one more big bottle, that'd make it thirty-seven cents." He frowned. "It doesn't come out right. We'd still have a penny left over."

"So let's quit now and settle for eleven cents each," Nick insisted.

"Ya dumb bunny, I said it won't work out to that.

It's ten cents each and two pennies left over."

"So we'll choose up for the two pennies. Odd man gets both."

Hank and Nick put their hands behind their backs, but Jim shook his head. "I don't want to quit now."

"That's the trouble with you, Jim. You never want to quit, and you think you can boss everybody. Well, you can't boss me, buster."

Jim, who did hate to quit, looked at Hank and saw that he was tending to go along with Nick.

"Okay, okay. We'll choose up for the extra two cents. But I'm not stopping. After we cash in these I'm gonna go to some more places, and I bet I get—I bet I get fifty cents by three o'clock."

"Huh," said Nick. "That'll be the day."

They chose for the two pennies, and Jim won, putting Nick in a worse mood, so that by the time they'd cashed in their ten bottles he wasn't speaking to Jim at all. Hank wavered between the two of them, but when he saw that Jim was determined to keep on bottle hunting, he went off with Nick.

Jim looked after them soberly. Quitters, that's what they were. Cruddy old quitters. He'd show them. He trudged down the street, stopped in front of a brand-new, huge apartment building and studied it thoughtfully. There was a doorman lounging against a wall just inside, and he gave Jim a narrow, suspicious look.

Boy, said Jim to himself. How do you like that?

Just for slowing down, he looks at me like that. He gave the doorman as insolent a return glance as he could manage, and it must have been pretty good because the guy actually showed signs of moving his fat feet and coming out.

Jim sauntered on, turned suddenly, and skipped down a passageway. As he'd thought, there was a service entrance back here. He looked around carefully, saw no one, and slipped inside. His heart pounded as he climbed the stairs. Not from exertion. From a nervous sense of wrongdoing. Only he couldn't figure out what he was doing that was wrong. Fooling that doorman wasn't. Fooling grown-ups like that doorman was part of the day's business. He decided he must be nervous because he'd never been in a building this fancy before.

His mouth felt suddenly dry as he came to the first door on the first floor. He couldn't ever remember feeling like this before, and he'd been bottle collecting for a couple of years now. Maybe Nick had been right. Maybe it'd be better to quit now, blow his twelve cents and have some fun. He realized with relief that no one was going to answer this door.

So now if he had the brains God gave a centipede, he'd get out of here. Even as he thought this, stubbornness forced him down the hall to the next door. Maybe they'd all be out. Maybe people in a place like this spent all their weekends at their country houses or something. So he'd ring two more doorbells, just to make it three, and he'd—

Before he could ring, the door suddenly opened and a man almost fell over him.

"What the— Who're you?"

"Nobody," Jim gulped. "I mean, I was just going."

"What brings you here to begin with? What's that bag for?"

Jim took a deep breath, and felt a sudden hard, almost unpleasant determination.

"Well, you see, mister," he said in his most coaxing, lost-boy tone, "I'm out trying to get deposit bottles that I can take back to the stores and make some money to get my little brother a birthday present. I mean, my old man's out of work, and this little brother of mine, Marshall his name is, he's only five, so he don't understand why he can't have no present, so I just thought—"

He could hardly believe the words as he heard them flow from his lips. Shame began to spread through him hotly. This wasn't like the other times, kidding people who maybe knew you were kidding, but doing it with Hank and Nick and doing it for kicks. This was—was *begging*. It was cheating and really lying. Using bad grammar on purpose to sound pathetic, saying those things about his *father*. He began to feel a little sick and could no longer meet the man's eyes.

"Son," said the man, "I don't know a thing about this bottle business, but here, take this—"

He shoved a dollar into Jim's hand and went down the hall without waiting for thanks. Jim stood frozen and helpless until he was out of sight. Then he looked down at the dollar. A dollar! It was crazy. He had an impulse to drop it on the floor. Or push it under the guy's door.

But a dollar . . .

He put it in his pocket and walked downstairs, biting his lip. He went back along the passageway, turned so he wouldn't have to pass that hotshot doorman again, and walked down the sunny street, lost in thought.

"Hey, Jim, where're you going?"

It was Hank, eating an ice cream cone. "You get that fifty cents yet, boy?"

Jim shook his head, without speaking.

"What's the matter with you?" Hank said. "You look funny. You spend your money yet?"

"No."

"Well, whyn't you get a cone, and we'll go over to the park and shoot marbles. You got any marbles with you?"

"No," Jim snapped. "Anyway I'm going home."

Hank looked startled. "Boy, you're in some mood today, I'll say."

"Well, say away. Only leave me alone, see?"

"I sure will, Jim boy. I sure enough will leave you alone."

Jim walked on, scowling and miserable, the dollar

like a burning spot in his pocket. He was so lost in puzzled thought that he didn't notice he was passing the shoe store where his father worked until a tap on the glass door reached his hearing. His father stood in there, waving at him, smiling that great smile, and for a second Jim was almost unable to wave back. He was ashamed to look at his father, whom he'd betrayed in such a way. He managed a wave and kept walking. Most times he'd have stopped for a second to talk or something. Not that Mr. Horney loved and encouraged that, but Papa would have wanted him to anyway.

Today he couldn't.

Mr. Davis remained at the door, looking after his son with a troubled expression. If Jim had been looking just ordinarily aggressive, he might not have noticed, since this boy of his, like many boys in the neighborhood, had a general air of "So you wanna fight, okay, let's fight." Mr. Davis wondered if this wasn't because so many of them looked at so much television. In television, the sides—good and evil— were clearly demarcated, but the solution for all problems, for both sides, was identical. Fight it out. I'm good, *bam,* I shoot you. I'm bad, *bam,* they got me. . . .

But Jim, just now, had looked not pugnacious but miserable. What, on a sunny Saturday, could be sending him down the street alone—he so rarely was alone—chewing his lip and staring in that fashion?

Mr. Davis opened the door and started out, full of concern.

"Davis! Davis! Where do you think you're going?"

Mr. Horney shot out of the stockroom, through the door, and onto the sidewalk in pursuit of his salesman. "Is it asking too much, *Mister* Davis, that you stay in the store during business hours and attend to business?"

Mr. Davis turned reluctantly. "Sorry, Mr. Horney. I just saw my son go by."

"I don't care if you saw your great grandfather's ghost go by. You chase your relatives *after* hours, do I make myself plain?"

"Of course."

" 'Of course,' he says. Of course." Mr. Horney muttered as they reentered the store. "Of course. Well, Mr. Of Course, would you be so kind as to go back there and check stock while I stay out here and try maybe to serve a customer, if a customer should come?"

"Of course," Mr. Davis said again, absentmindedly. He started off.

"Hey, Davis?"

"Yes, Mr. Horney?"

"Where's that, you know, sketch you were doing? Of me," he added, sounding suddenly shy. "You know, that drawing . . . of me."

"I have it over at my studio, transferring it to canvas." Tulio had given him an old canvas, and he was painting Mr. Horney's face—which was getting more and more interesting from an artistic point of view—over what had been a still life of decayed fruit that Tulio had entitled "Horrorscape with Bananas" and had gotten tired of.

"That's what you're doing, eh?" Mr. Horney looked down demurely. Then he glanced up and said, "Studio? You've got a *studio*, yet? You tell me you can't afford shoes for your kids and I should give them to you wholesale—which I'll do if you're ever able to pay even wholesale—and all the time you've got a—"

"No, no," Mr. Davis interrupted. "I didn't mean that, not exactly. This friend of mine, over on West Thirteenth, he has the studio. He lets me use a corner of it, that's all. And I've been painting your portrait," he went on hastily. "When I have some paints, that is. And the time, of course. I only paint on Sunday, because of course the job comes first. You have a very interesting face from the artist's point of view, Mr. Horney."

"I do, do I?" said Mr. Horney. He turned away and began to rearrange a display of cork-soled wedgies. After a moment Mr. Davis went into the stockroom and tried to remember what he was supposed to be doing there.

He couldn't see where in that conversation he could have worked in his idea, which was that he paint the portrait in exchange for shoes for his family. Plainly Mr. Horney was fascinated at the idea of having his portrait painted, but he might not be so fascinated to exchange it for real goods. Especially not when he saw it.

It was somewhat later, when Mr. Horney was out getting a Coke, that the vast customer came in. She was so big that Mr. Davis blinked in pure admiration. Like a California redwood, she loomed into the little store and stood there as solid as something planted centuries before.

"My word," said Mr. Davis. "May I help you, madam?"

"I want to see a pair of sandals. Pink ones."

"Pink sandals." Mr. Davis glanced professionally toward her feet. "About a size ten and a half?" he guessed.

The woman's eyes sparkled. "Nine," she said firmly. "I wear a size nine."

Mr. Davis closed his mouth on a protest, went toward the shelf of sandals. "Flat heels?" he asked.

"Certainly not. I'm not wearing flat heels now, am I?"

"No. No, you aren't," said Mr. Davis with respect. "But I just thought, in a sandal . . ."

"Don't think. Just show me some size nine pink sandals with high heels."

Miraculously there was just such a pair, with elastic straps for the heel, so that, in a sense, the customer was able to get her big shapely feet into them.

She stood, teetered, walked over to a mirror, and said, "What do you think?"

Mr. Davis, artist, not Mr. Davis, shoe salesman, looked at the general effect and shook his head. The huge feet were wedged between slender straps, and they thrust downward from spindly heels so that all ten toes were touching the floor.

"Terrible," he said sincerely. "They look awful."

"Say, you've got some nerve! What kind of a salesman are you anyway?"

Mr. Horney, coming in the door at that moment, grew red with rage and answered, "He's a no-good salesman, that's the kind of a salesman he is, and I'm here to tell you so. May I present myself, madam. I am the founder of this business, and the—"

"What've you got him here for, then, if you know what kind a salesman he is, that's what I'd like to know. Do you know what he said?" she demanded. "He says these shoes look terrible on me."

"Madam, I apologize. I deeply, deeply apologize. He has no taste and of course the shoes look perfect on you. Dainty and becoming." He shot a glance at Mr. Davis. "And you're fired, see? As of last week."

"But—"

"No buts. Just beat it before I have a heart attack."

"But Mr. Horney—"

"Davis, I don't want to call the cops on you, but if you don't go *this* minute—"

Mr. Davis frowned, sighed, attempted to speak

again, thought better of it, and left.

He walked home slowly and climbed the stairs with an effort, hoping everyone would be out. If he could just sit quietly by himself for a while and think, maybe he'd find some way to tell his family. If he could just—

But they were all there. Jim playing moodily with a deck of cards, Franny and Marshall studying her scrapbook, Mrs. Davis humming as she prepared a meat loaf in the kitchen. Everyone looked around at his step, but only Marshall spoke.

"Papa!" he said happily. "You're home early!"

Jim, Franny, and Mrs. Davis said nothing out loud. In three pairs of eyes he read the words "You've been fired again."

He nodded as if they'd spoken, and moved Fudge out of his chair so he could sit down.

Fudge had been playing with something and now he tapped it across the floor. It rolled toward Marshall and the scrapbook.

"Hey," said Marshall. "Lookit! Fudge found a dollar!"

"He what?" said Mrs. Davis without expression.

"A dollar," Marshall said brightly. He picked up the crumpled bill and smoothed it out. "Isn't he a smart cat to do that?"

"Where could that have come from?" said Mr. Davis.

Franny and Jim shook their heads, and neither Mr.

nor Mrs. Davis noticed that while Franny just looked interested, Jimmy's expression was nervous and defiant.

Mrs. Davis said wearily, "You just must have dropped it sometime, that's all."

"Who can drop a dollar and not notice?" He exhaled a long breath, handed her the dollar, and said, "Well, it'll come in handy."

"Oh, yes. It'll come in handy."

Jimmy got to his feet, brushed his hands on his pants legs, and said, "Anything I can do to help with dinner, huh?"

Franny told herself that it was not nice to be annoyed with him. But it was as if his offer underlined the fact that they were all in trouble again. When things were going well, Jimmy didn't bother to make himself useful.

Chapter Eight

Franny didn't see Simone all weekend. Usually on Sunday either Simone came to her apartment or she went to Simone's, but today Franny felt she should stay with her family.

When Papa lost a job, a terrible sort of sadness came down over things. In some way that she couldn't explain to herself, Franny felt that by staying close, by talking and making herself loudly present, it helped to make something awful seem less awful.

Jim had been up and out of the house practically at dawn, and Marshall, happy not to have to go across the hall to Mrs. Mundy, was content just to be with his parents. He sat beside his father while Mr. Davis went up and down every column of the *Help Wanted: Male* section of the paper. Marshall looked at the big print, picked out the letters he knew, and announced them loudly.

"That's one of mine," he said to his father. "That's a *G*. And that's a *A* and that's a *E* and that's a—" He frowned and fell silent.

"Hmm?" said Mr. Davis absently. "You stuck, Marsh?"

"No."

"Good." Mr. Davis started to turn the page.

"It's a *J!*" Marshall shouted.

Franny came over and patted him on the head. "You see," she said. "You learned it after all. It wasn't so bad, was it?" Her voice was strained and gay. It was a tone meant to disguise a feeling within her. A sort of cold, end-of-the-world feeling that came from knowing Papa was scared and trying not to show it.

"Here's something," Mr. Davis called out. "There's a job here for—Oh, no. Have to be a college graduate."

"What's a college graduate?" Marshall asked.

"A person who went to college and got a degree," Franny explained.

"What's a degree?"

"What you get when you go to college."

"And Papa hasn't got one?"

"No," said Mr. Davis. "Papa hasn't got one."

"Why not?" said Marshall.

"Because I didn't go to college."

"Why not?"

"Because I didn't have the money to go."

Marshall thought he finally had the answer to that. "But now you have," he said. "You have the dollar Fudge found."

Mr. Davis gave a half laugh. "It takes a bit more than that."

"How much?"

"Marshall, stop," said Franny. "It takes lots and lots of money to go to college. And besides, Papa's too old now."

For a second Mr. Davis looked hurt, but then he gave his half laugh again and jumped to his feet. "Let's all go out and take a walk, eh? It's too dark and stuffy in here."

Marshall sprang up, but Mrs. Davis, who was doing housecleaning, shook her head. Franny decided to stay with her mother and help. "I know," she said, with the first gleam of pleasure she'd felt in hours, "I know, Mama. Let's change the furniture around."

Mr. Davis laughed out loud. "Franny," he said, "I do believe that if you were in charge of a graveyard, you'd move all the tombstones around once a month."

"But it's fun!" Franny said loudly, trying to drive the sound of the words *graveyard, tombstones,* out of her mind. "It's *fun.* See, Mama, we could move the sofa over by that wall there and then if we put Papa's chair sort of out in the middle of the room instead of stuck in the corner—"

"Franny, for goodness' sake," Mrs. Davis began a bit sharply, "haven't we enough trouble without—" But she broke off and smiled faintly. "All right. Maybe it would be sort of cheery at that. Anything for a change, is that it?"

Franny noticed that her parents weren't looking at each other. All morning, when they'd spoken, it had sort of been through either her or Marshall. They'd never looked right at each other and said anything. Her parents never really quarreled, shouting and carrying on the way some people did. The Orgellas, for instance. When *they* were all together, they battled around a good deal. But Franny hated it when the air got cold this way with her parents' silence toward each other.

After Papa had gone out with Marshall, Franny made a listless effort to interest her mother again in furniture rearranging but gave up quickly. Mrs. Davis looked as if she were just about to cry but didn't intend to. Franny knew the feeling. She knew that words, especially nice words, made the tears come. So she said nothing for a long time. She cleaned the bathroom, giving it an extra hard scrubbing, and then did the bedroom, playing for a while with Fudge, who loved to chase a finger moving under blankets.

By the time she came out of the bedroom, hungry for lunch, her mother seemed to be feeling better. They had crackers with melted cheese on them, and for dessert crackers with marshmallows melted on them. That had been an invention of Jimmy's. A little spot of jam, a marshmallow, and into the oven for a toasting.

"It's good," Franny said, licking her fingers. "Isn't it? Jimmy's not so dumb all the time."

"No," said Mrs. Davis. "Neither are you."

Franny gave her mother a quick glance. After a second they smiled, and for the first time since last night Franny felt a little warmth, a touch of confidence.

"Papa will find a job, won't he?" she said. "A job better even than that old shoe store one, won't he, don't you think?"

After a long pause Mrs. Davis said, "Well, he'll have to find one, won't he?"

This wasn't what Franny had wanted at all. She wished she hadn't spoken but had just hugged that smile and moment of warmth close, because now they were gone again, and now it seemed worse than before. She tried to swallow away a painful feeling in her throat so as to start a new conversation about something else. Not about moving the furniture around, because she didn't feel much like doing that anymore. Not about Marshall's birthday, because that would only make them more upset. Well, but there must be *something* to talk about. If that pain in her throat would just *stop*—

"Where's Simone?" Mrs. Davis said suddenly, and Franny burst into tears.

It was, in a way, the most beautiful relief. The ache flowed out of her throat, and when Mama came and held her close she had a floating, sweet sensation that all in the world that mattered was to have her mother's arms holding her while she cried. Even after she couldn't force out any more tears, she still stayed close to her mother, leaning against her.

"Did you quarrel?" Mrs. Davis asked, pushing her daughter's damp hair away from the wide forehead. Franny nodded. "What about, Franny?"

"Oh—" Franny struggled up, wiping her eyes. "She said I was ugly."

Mrs. Davis looked astonished. "But she—she couldn't have. Franny, now try to be honest. That couldn't have been what she said. Simone is your friend. And besides, you're pretty."

"Am I?" Franny said faintly. "Oh, well . . . she said I looked ugly because of what I was doing."

"What were you doing?"

"I was only picking a scab off my knee," Franny

burst out. "What's so awful about that? That Simone, she wants the whole entire world to look like a picture of something. She wants everything to be so *pretty*. Well, everything isn't pretty all the time, that's all."

"No," Mrs. Davis said sadly. "No, everything isn't pretty all the time. You mean that's all? That was the whole quarrel?"

"I don't know," Franny said in a dismal tone. "Maybe. Francisco came back then, and we, Simone and I, we never did talk again. I *hate* not talking with people. Like," she went on recklessly, "I hate how you and Papa don't talk to each other when— when something goes wrong." Her mother's face got quite still, but Franny could not be stopped now. "People who don't talk to each other—I think it's worse than yelling. I do, I do . . ." By now she was yelling herself, and close to tears again.

Mrs. Davis leaned over and kissed her gently. "You're quite right," she said.

Franny blinked in surprise. Sweet and dear as her mother was, she was also usually pretty stern, especially when things were going wrong. Like the time the telephone company took their phone away. No one, not even Jimmy, had dared to say a word because of the look on Mama's face.

"Now," said Mrs. Davis, "why don't you rinse your face off, and then go around to Simone's?"

"Why doesn't she come here?" Franny demanded.

"Maybe she's waiting for you to go there. When there's been a misunderstanding, Franny, somebody has to make the first move. Somebody has to be generous and big."

Franny debated, shook her head. "I want to stay with you. I love being with you." Especially she loved it now, when she felt so close to her mother and had her all to herself.

Down in the street a siren wailed, going past with a lifting shriek, disappearing with a long-drawn-out moan. Franny shuddered as its terrible, mysterious message reached her ears.

"Mama," she said suddenly, "Mama—do you know, sometimes I get awfully scared."

"Of what, Franny?"

"Of"—she drew a deep, strangled breath and got the word out—"of dying."

Mrs. Davis looked into the pinched, anxious face. "Must you think about it?" she said at length, helplessly. "You're so young. And healthy."

"It isn't me I'm afraid for," Franny said urgently. "Or, anyway, not just for me. Not mostly for me." The truth was she almost never thought about herself and dying. "It's—it's you and Papa," she said in a rush. "I get so scared that maybe you or Papa will—" But she couldn't say it again. "Mama, could you promise me you won't? Couldn't you promise me?"

Again Mrs. Davis took a while before speaking. "Franny, don't you see that promises are for—*prom-*

ise is a meaningless word. People getting married promise each other to be happy forever. People promise to respect a certain idea forever. They must know these aren't things they can guarantee, no matter how much they want to. Sometimes I think the word is just useless. You can't promise anything that matters, and if it doesn't matter, why use such an important word?"

"But Mama!" Franny cried out desperately. "Mama, you have to!"

Suddenly Mrs. Davis opened her arms and Franny fled into them.

"All right, my love. Insofar as a human being can make a promise, I promise that your father and I will live to see you children grown up."

At the words Franny felt a peculiar ease flowing through her, even as she knew that what her mother had said was true, that that kind of promise cannot be made.

"I'll give you something more practical than a promise," Mrs. Davis said, "and that is that your father and I have a lot to live for. You'll find as you get older, Franny, that having a lot to live for is a better guarantee of long life than promises can be."

"But he got *sick*," Franny cried out, the sense of reassurance already beginning to ebb. "Why did he get so sick?"

"Oh, Franny, Franny . . . He got better, didn't he? He's fine now."

There was that touch of sternness, of hardness, in her mother's voice that warned Franny not to go on with her questions, her demands. Yet Mrs. Davis's words were still gentle, and she kissed her daughter's cheek lovingly.

Franny pushed her hair back and moved out of her mother's arms, knowing she'd gotten, for now, all the help that was possible. It wasn't enough, but still it had helped.

"Let's move the furniture around," she said, wanting to be doing something, wanting to talk of unimportant things. "Let's put Papa's chair right in the middle of the room, so it will look sort of like—as if we had loads of space and could put a chair anywhere."

"How will we get around it?" Mrs. Davis said with a laugh. But she followed Franny to the chair and they began to tug it out of the corner toward the center of the room.

"Well," Franny conceded, "maybe we'll have to put it back when we're done. But let's *start* this way."

They were still at it when Jim came in demanding lunch, and instead of snorting and asking if Franny was ever going to give up her dopey ideas, he pitched in and helped to shove and pull the furniture.

What a peculiar thing, Franny said to herself. How funny it is that when something awful happens, like Papa getting sick or losing his job, Jimmy and I seem to get nicer to each other, when most of the time we aren't nice at all. It's a shame we can't be this way all the time, she thought, looking at her brother, who gave her a sweaty smile as he wrestled with the sofa-bed.

When Marshall and his father got downstairs, the bells of St. Anthony of Padua were striking the hour.

One . . . two . . . three . . . It got past ten and, as usual, Marshall lost count. But it didn't matter as long as he could skip along beside his father. While Marshall did not know just what was involved in losing a job, he knew his father had lost one. He also knew that it wasn't quite as cheery around the house this morning as he liked it to be. Even Franny wasn't humming or anything.

But here, now, with Papa, everything was fine.

They didn't hurry. They dawdled. They looked in the shops. There were beautiful things in some of the windows, and the Chinese laundry had wind chimes hanging in the doorway, turning and tinkling. They stopped in front of the Mexican store. SALE! said a fancy sign that Papa read aloud to him. SALE OF GLORIOUS MEXICAN HANDICRAFTS.

"My friend Tulio lettered that sign," said Papa.

Marshall was impressed. "It's pretty," he said. "Those little snakes and things, and the flowers. When people make a sale, what happens?"

"People who buy the things save money."

"Then why don't we buy something and save some money?" Marshall asked, trying to be helpful. It seemed a good idea, but Papa only laughed.

"We don't have any money to save." He said the customary words in a jovial fashion.

Mr. Davis was a man who believed in putting unpleasant things out of mind as much as possible. Having done what he could for today about finding a job, having gone carefully through the want ad section of the paper and marked off some likely and unlikely prospects for looking into tomorrow, he now proposed to forget the whole business. Up in the apartment there, with his wife so silent and Franny so tense, to forget had been a bit difficult. Down here in the street with Marshall it was no problem.

They strode along together, breathing deeply of the air which was warm but laced with autumn sparkle. They talked of this and that, of people they passed, about plans for trips they might one day take. Marshall was all for going to Africa, where he could sit in a tree and look at lions and gorillas, but Mr. Davis thought they should see their own American West first. Marshall finally agreed.

Time passed happily, and it was well into the afternoon before they realized that they were hungry.

"I'll tell you what," said Mr. Davis. "Let's go up and see Tulio." There was just a chance that Tulio might have some bread and salami to spare. Anyway there'd be the smell of paint and turpentine and canvas. Mr. Davis felt he couldn't go another hour without that odor to sustain him.

"Come on, Marshall," he said. "Let's hurry."

When Marshall ran beside his father, he did not get a stitch in his side. He just bounded along like a rabbit. They were bowling down the street together, merry as could be, when Marshall saw Francisco.

"Hey, Papa," he said, drawing to a stop. "There's Francisco."

"Ah?" said Mr. Davis. "Where?" And then, "Who's Francisco?"

"My friend."

"I remember. Simone's cousin from San Juan."

"Yes," said Marshall. "Francisco."

By now Francisco was upon them and almost past before he noticed Marshall beaming up at him. He stopped, and he and Mr. Davis said what a pleasure it was to meet and how pleasant the weather was, and then Francisco, who wasn't going anywhere in particular, went along with them to Tulio's studio.

It developed that Tulio had more than salami and bread. He had cheese and fruit and wine. He even had cocoa for Marshall.

Tulio, in fact, had sold another painting.

"And that, my friends," he said, slapping his thigh, "makes two paintings I have sold. One five years ago and one the day before yesterday. That does not, you may point out, establish a trend, but it's heartening, most heartening. Which is why we are all eating so well, and I'm very glad you stopped by to celebrate."

"So also am I, señor," said Francisco, just as Mr. Davis said, "Anytime, anytime."

Marshall stirred his cocoa and smiled. He liked this place, with its great grimy skylight and the long, long room in which there was just about no furniture at all. Just Tulio's bed, his table with paints on it, lots of wooden crates, his easel and chair, and a huge, high, heavy piece of furniture that Papa said was called a wardrobe. Tulio kept his clothes in it. Way down at the other end of the room were Papa's easel and chair. Papa's paints—he didn't have many— were on top of an upended crate.

When he'd had enough to eat, Marshall wandered down the long room to see what Papa was painting. After him came Tulio, Francisco, and finally Papa himself. They all looked at the portrait of Mr. Horney.

"I began," Mr. Davis said thoughtfully, "by calling it 'Sell More Shoes.' "

"What do you call it now?" Francisco asked, studying the face in the painting.

"Now I call it 'Loneliness.' "

Tulio and Francsico nodded.

Mr. Horney's face looked mournfully out of the canvas, with a wrinkled, testy, very sad expression.

"Why is he green?" Marshall asked. "Is that the color of his face?"

"It's the color of his soul," said Mr. Davis. "He

has a somber, greenish-gray soul, and that's what came out in the painting."

Tulio stood back a bit, squinting one eye at the canvas. "Still, there is something good in that face."

"Oh, yes, yes," said Mr. Davis. "Mr. Horney is a good man. Sorely tried, sorely tried. But a good man."

"Who is this gentleman?" said Francisco. "A friend?"

"No. My employer. At least he was my employer until yesterday."

"Did you get fired again?" Tulio asked, and when Mr. Davis nodded, he said, "What a terrible business this is. An artist trying to work in a shoe store. You might as well put a giraffe in a closet and tell him it's his native plain."

Marshall laughed at this.

"I think it would be fun," Francisco was saying wistfully. "To work in a store and meet all the people and smell the good leather. I should think—"

"Francisco!" said Mr. Davis. "Francisco, I have an idea. I only got fired yesterday, and Mr. Horney can't have found another clerk yet. Maybe if we go around to where he lives and see him—" He broke off. "No, I guess not."

"Why not?" Francisco pressed eagerly. "I assure you, señor, I would work very hard for this Mr. Horney."

"Oh, it isn't that, and I'm sure you would. I just

don't think that my recommendation would do you any good."

"Papa says he couldn't get the president of the United States a job," Marshall said proudly.

Francisco's eyes grew bleak. "If you say so, señor." He turned away and walked slowly down the room.

Mr. Davis and Tulio frowned at each other.

"I suppose it couldn't do any harm to try," Mr. Davis said.

"That's right," said Tulio.

"I could take him the portrait, as a gift. As a souvenir of our acquaintance."

Tulio looked mistrustfully at the face on the canvas. "Does he appreciate art, this Mr. Horney? Or does he like pretty pictures?"

"Only one way to find out," said Mr. Davis, lifting the picture off the easel. He shook his head morosely. "My last canvas."

"I'll give you another," said Tulio. "In celebration. It is also an old one," he added, "that you can paint over." As Tulio and Mr. Davis were always painting new pictures over old ones, this was immaterial, and Mr. Davis accepted gratefully.

Chapter Nine

Francisco, Marshall, and Mr. Davis walked around to the apartment building where Mr. Horney lived alone. They were glad to find him in, as on such a beautiful day it seemed more likely to them that he would have been out.

Mr. Horney, however, rarely went out, since he could never decide where to go. He was a lonely, shy man, and the only place he felt comfortable and correct was in his shoe store. There he was the boss.

Everywhere else as soon as he got there it occurred to him that he didn't belong and all the people knew it and were waiting for him to leave.

Today when his doorbell rang, he was so surprised that at first he didn't answer. At the second ring he opened the door and found, to his astonishment, his ex-salesman, a little boy, and a tall, tan young man with eager eyes.

"Well, my goodness," said Mr. Horney. "What is this?" He looked at what Mr. Davis was carrying, guessing in a flash just what it was.

"It's a silverneer," said Marshall, but so low that nobody heard him.

"Come in, come in," said Mr. Horney excitedly. "Come in." He gestured toward a chair. "Put it there," he said to Mr. Davis. "I want to look at it." He looked for a long, long time. "Well," he said at last. "That is how you see me." From his voice there was no way to tell whether he was pleased or displeased.

Mr. Davis couldn't think of anything to say, and he was hoping Marshall wouldn't be able to either, when Francisco spoke up.

"A portrait painter, señor, paints an atmosphere as well as a form. A green atmosphere about a man would indicate that he was woodsy and reflective, would it not? At least this is what I would take it to mean."

The words appealed to Mr. Horney. Woodsy and reflective. They sounded cool and refreshing. Put that way, he began to see the portrait as Francisco did. The green, which had seemed at first rather bean-soupy, took on a forest tinge and the face itself became that of a hermit, a man who dwelt alone in deep places. All in all, the more he looked, the more he liked what he saw.

"Well, now," he said, turning to Mr. Davis. "You surely didn't bring this to me as a present." No one ever gave Mr. Horney presents, and he was confident that a fired shoe salesman would not be the one to start. "You'd like to sell it to me, right?" His face took on a bargaining, you-aren't-going-to-get-around-me expression.

Mr. Davis, who'd been planning to ask for some shoes in return for the picture, all at once decided that a gesture was called for. He was a man who liked to make gestures but was rarely in a position to do so.

"Not at all, not at all," he said now. "I have always intended to give it to you, Mr. Horney." This was true. He'd intended to give it in exchange for something, but *had* intended to give it. "I am only happy if it pleases you."

Mr. Horney was quite taken aback. "You mean it?" he said. "Just as a—as a gift? Why, my goodness, Mr. Davis, I don't know what to say." He began to feel a little embarrassed. "I do suppose that if you want to come back—that is, come back and try—I mean to say—"

He was out of his depth. He did not want the

unreliable and eccentric Mr. Davis back in his shoe store. Not in the least. On the other hand, here he had been given this handsome present of a portrait—and the more he looked the more taken he was with this hermitlike version of his face and character—so that some offer in return seemed called for. He was unhappy and looked it.

"That's considerate of you, Mr. Horney," said Mr. Davis, coming to his rescue. "But the fact is—" He'd been about to say he had another job—not as a matter of face-saving, since to him pride was not involved, but just to make things less awkward. However he didn't want to lie, and besides he could scarcely have found a job since yesterday afternoon. "The fact is," he said, "that I don't feel I make a good shoe salesman."

Mr. Horney nodded vigorous agreement.

"On the other hand," Mr. Davis went on, "and if you haven't already replaced me—" Mr. Horney's heart sank, but he shook his head. "Then I do have a suggestion, which is that Señor Orgella here, who is a lover of fine leather, be offered a chance at the position." He stopped, feeling pleased with the dignified way in which he'd put this.

Mr. Horney scrutinized Francisco. "Where are you from?" he said at length.

"San Juan, señor."

"You speak Spanish of course."

"*Sí*, señor."

"Well, but this may be just the answer. This may

be an excellent thought indeed, Davis. As you know, we have a great many Spanish-speaking people moving to our part of the city, and what could be better than to have someone who speaks the language right there in the store to help them?"

"That's very true," said Mr. Davis, "Very true. You might put a sign in the window saying, 'Here we speak Spanish.' "

"A sign in the window. Of course," said Mr. Horney. "But I also," he said with a proud, mysterious air, "intend to put something else in the window." He swept a hand toward the portrait. "What do you think, Mr. Davis?"

"The portrait? In your store window?"

"Just so. With, I think, a tastefully lettered sign beneath, saying SAMUEL EGGERSTON HORNEY, FOUNDER." He'd founded his store two years ago, but decided to leave that information out.

"Why—why, I think that would be splendid, splendid," said Mr. Davis, wishing he'd signed his name in larger letters. He could hardly suggest to Mr. Horney that the artist's name be included on the tastefully lettered sign, and clearly all Mr. Horney was concerned with was having his portrait, in oil, with Samuel Eggerston Horney, Founder, there in the window for all to see. "Splendid," he repeated.

Mr. Horney beamed upon the painting. Marshall shifted restlessly. Francisco smiled from face to face. At length Mr. Davis said, "Well, we may take it that it's all settled, then?"

There was a rising "Hmm?" from the shoe store founder.

"Mr. Horney?" said Mr. Davis, more loudly.

"Yes. Yes, what is it, Davis?"

"Señor Orgella. Should he report for work in the morning?"

"By all means. I said so, didn't I? Now, about having the signs lettered—"

"My friend Tulio can do that for you. He's a letterer. Very inexpensive and good. He's also an artist, of course, but a letterer in his spare time."

"Oh, good," said Mr. Horney. "Have him do a high-class job, mind."

"The best."

Their parting was as high-hearted as anyone could have wished, and as Marshall and his father mounted the stairs back home, Mr. Davis was whistling with good humor.

"Papa got a job! Papa got a job!" Marshall shouted the moment they stepped in the door. He didn't have a chance to add that the job was for Francisco. To Marshall, in fact, it was not important who had gotten the job. He just wanted to start telling about his exciting afternoon and these were the words he chose to begin with.

"Why, how wonderful, how marvelous," said Mrs. Davis. "But how did you ever—and on a Sunday afternoon—why, I don't know what to say."

"Papa, Papa," screamed Franny. "Oh, you're so

smart, my Papa. There's nobody in the world as
smart as you!"

Jim was nodding agreement when Mr. Davis, his
whistling mood quite vanished, said, "Marshall has
jumped the gun a bit. That is to say, I did, in a
manner of speaking, get a job. Only I didn't get it for
myself."

"Not for yourself?" said Mrs. Davis.

"Oh, Papa." Franny sighed.

"How do you get a job not for yourself?" said
Jim.

Mr. Davis sat down to explain, and somehow, here

with his family, the triumph of the afternoon seemed dim and hollow. Franny was pleased that now Francisco had a job. Mrs. Davis was trying to be pleased and probably was, but to be pleased and disappointed at once puts a strain on the disposition. Jim kicked the sofa leg and didn't even pretend to care about Francisco.

By the time Mr. Davis got to the part about a painting by him hanging in the shoe store window for all to see, nobody seemed much impressed. Mrs. Davis and Jim just looked at him, and even Franny only managed a short "How nice for you, Papa."

Mr. Davis picked up the newspaper and began going through the columns again so he wouldn't have to look at anybody anymore. Marshall took Fudge and went to bed right after dinner without being asked. He fell asleep immediately. Jim and Franny did their homework in silence and retired. After a while, in silence, Mr. and Mrs. Davis went to bed too.

But it's funny, Franny thought again just before she fell asleep, how awful it is when nobody's talking. It seemed ages since she'd really talked with anyone, and suppose tomorrow Simone didn't talk to her either. For the first time she began to understand how truly terrible it must have been for the Little Mermaid to lose her voice and the company of all her gay and chattering sisters.

Silence can be so lonely.

Chapter Ten

That Sunday afternoon Simone had taken the old battered baby buggy out so that José could have an hour in the sun, but a wheel had come off, so she'd been forced to pull it back and sit on the stoop while two of her brothers attempted to fix it. They hadn't done a good job, and finally Simone had carried José back upstairs, giving up hope of getting to Washington Square that day.

It had taken her longer to give up hope that

Franny would come around to visit. Of course she could have asked Grandmother to watch José for a while and then gone to see Franny herself, but she kept putting it off. By the time it was late afternoon and her parents got home from visiting uptown, she was so put out that she didn't want to go anywhere.

"Did Franny come by today?" said Mrs. Orgella.

Simone scowled and said she didn't know or care where Franny was.

"*Muchacha*," said Mrs. Orgella. "What has got into you?"

"Nothing at all," said Simone airily. "I'm only saying that I haven't the least interest in Franny Davis. She thinks she's so much *smarter* than everybody else."

"I think maybe she is, too," said Mrs. Orgella, laughing. But she saw immediately that Simone was in no mood for humor. "Poor little one," she said lovingly. "You do not have enough time for yourself. Why don't you run out now and play. I will take care of José, and I will force your brothers to set the table for you tonight. So, you are free until dinnertime."

Simone hesitated. She had nowhere special to go, but didn't get a chance like this often. Giving her mother a quick kiss, she ran downstairs past her brothers, who shouted after her that she should go back and help get dinner.

Around the corner, she slowed down. If she kept on going this way, she would come first to Lila

Wembleton's, and then if she kept going even far-
ther, to Franny's. It was a question of whether she
wanted to see either of them, and she decided probably she did, only since she was mad at both of them
it was a matter of deciding which one to make up
with first.

She struck a bargain with herself. If Lila was outside, that would be a sign. So she'd stay and see her.
If she wasn't . . . well, said Simone to herself, then I'll
walk over Franny's way and *maybe* go upstairs. She
didn't really see why she should be the first to give
in. By now she couldn't recall what it was that had
gotten her and Franny mad at each other this time,
but of course it must have been Franny's fault.

Lila was on the steps of her father's house playing
jacks. She brightened when she saw Simone. "Hi,"
she said. "Where did you come from?"

Simone could remember longer than most when
she had had a falling out with someone. Where Lila
or Franny forgot if they weren't reminded, Simone
could recall the smallest slight. Or if she couldn't
recall the actual slight, could always remember that
she'd felt it. Most of the time she was willing to make
up, especially with Franny.

The first day Francisco had met Franny he'd said
later, "That is the kind of young lady you make
friends with and when you're an old lady, there you
will be—still friends. She has quality." People were
always *praising* Franny.

Simone decided to stay with Lila, who had comfortable faults. She picked up the ball and the jacks and began her faultless game.

"Where's Ginny?" she said after a while.

"Her?" Lila said coolly. "I'm here to say I *don't* know. My mother told me not to have anything to do with her anymore. My mother says they have cockroaches in their kitchen."

Simone started to say, "So have we," changed it to, "Franny's brother Jimmy says that it's mankind against the insects now, and the insects are winning."

"You will kindly not talk about Fran Davis *or* her ghastly brother," directed Lila, putting the jacks away without asking if Simone wanted to stop. She certainly didn't like losing at games.

It's no wonder she goes through her friends so fast, Simone thought. But still she stayed. They went in after a while and had some ginger ale and cookies and then went into Lila's room.

As Simone had told Franny, this was a room full of fancy, pretty things. Each time she came Simone seemed to find something more to envy. Today it was a milk-blue china cat reposing on the dressing table with the pink flouncy skirt. Simone looked at the cat for a long time. It was awfully, awfully nice.

But still, neither the china cat nor the whole rest of the room ever made her ache with that strange lonely feeling that she got sometimes when something seemed to her truly beautiful. To try to make the feeling clear, she called it a headache or a stomachache. But it was neither of these. It was some-thing . . . something . . . She almost knew but could never put into words what it was. It was like trying to explain a thing in Spanish, a language she only almost knew. Sometimes when Francisco talked, seeming so happy in the hot bright words of Puerto Rico, Simone wished her own parents hadn't all but given it up.

"I think I'll learn Spanish," she said now to Lila.

"Why, for goodness' sake? Anyway I thought you already knew it."

"No. Only a little. My parents speak just Ameri-can."

"English," Lila corrected.

"American. It's different from English."

Lila shrugged. "It's hard enough learning English-American, without adding Spanish. Don't you just hate grammar? Isn't that grisliest?"

"I hate arithmetic more."

"Oh, I hate that too. As a matter of fact, I hate school, of course there are boys there, and that helps. I'm getting to the boy-crazy stage," Lila added proudly.

"You are?"

"Oh, yes. I think about boys most of the time. And there's a fellow in my class who notices me. A lot." Lila picked up one of her toy stuffed animals, a dog with trailing legs, and hugged it close. "Isn't it going to be scrumptious, Simone?"

"What's going to be?"

"Oh, *all* of it. Boys and dates and kissing and everything. I just can hardly wait."

"Let's play some records."

"Okay."

Presently Lila lifted her voice above a moaning quartet. "How come you aren't with Franny Davis today, huh?"

"I thought you didn't want to talk about her."

"I don't. I just wondered, that's all."

"She's not the only friend I have, you know."

"*If* she's a friend," Lila said with a sideways glance.

"What's that supposed to mean?"

"Nothing. Absolutely nothing. Only if somebody talked about me, I'm not sure I'd be so anxious to call her my friend."

"Talked about me *how?* I haven't done anything," said Simone, but she began to feel a little cold. Franny couldn't, she *wouldn't* have told anyone about that—that note she'd sent to Mr. Ferris, the phys ed teacher? I wouldn't do something like that to her, Simone thought. Only, of course, perfect *Franny* would never write a silly, crazy letter like that. Oh, but she'd never *tell*, Simone assured herself again. "I don't know what you're talking about Lila. And I don't think you do either."

Lila turned the record. "Maybe not." She started talking about boys again and about how they noticed her, and shortly Simone left for home.

She imagined that one day a conversation about boys would interest her very much. Her own sister Consuelo, who wasn't fourteen yet, talked about nothing else. And all Consuelo's friends were the same. But my goodness, Simone said to herself now, what a dope that Lila is. Boys *noticing* her. I'll bet. And Franny just isn't the sort of person who goes around saying things about her friends. Especially not about something like that letter, which had been told to her in the strictest secrecy. Simone's cheeks burned at the thought that by now everyone in class could know. Oh, why, why, had she ever written it? It was just because he was so handsome and so nice. But the *things* she'd said . . .

On the stairway behind her there was a light step and Francisco came up whistling, taking the steps two at a time.

"Hello, Francisco," she said gloomily. "Boy, you look happy."

"Do I?" said Francisco. "Well, that's because I am."

"Why?" Simone demanded. Since the day he'd come from San Juan, she'd never seen her cousin looking like this. "Did somebody leave you a million dollars?"

"Why," said Francisco, "should it be that if a person looks happy in this country, somebody always asks if he's been left a million dollars? Is money the only reason for a man to whistle? Why do you not say, 'Francisco, have you inherited a star? Have you unearthed a treasure chest containing affection and grace?' Why doesn't anyone say, 'Francisco, have you fallen in love?' Why money, Simone? Why always money?"

A little hurt, Simone said, "I suppose it's because that's what most grown-up people talk about."

"Oh, now. I've wounded you. Come, Simone, forgive me. And you are quite right, of course. Money is what everyone talks of. It's also what everyone needs, let us have no mistake about that. I just get tired, sometimes, hearing about it. Ah . . . what delicious odors are wafting toward us!"

"Why so peppy, Francisco?" said Mr. Orgella. "Somebody die and leave you a million?"

Francisco winked at Simone and picked up his guitar and sang about a man who died in happy torment for love of an icy lady.

Francisco's first wish had been to rush back to this crowded living room and announce his triumph. But as soon as he had parted from Mr. Davis and that most agreeable Marshall, he'd begun to get a dreamlike feeling. Had he, in truth, been offered a job by the founder of a shoe store, in that very founder's apartment? Could it be so? He decided that on the whole it would be best to say nothing at all. Tomorrow he would go to that shoe store the very first thing in the morning and present himself to Mr. Horney. If Mr. Horney didn't look at him and say,

"Look here, señor, can't you take a joke? You didn't think I was serious, did you?" If, in fact, Mr. Horney said, "Ah, there you are," and took him inside and showed him all the shoes and said, "Now, señor, sell them. In both American and Spanish," and if, further, he, Francisco, were still in that store at the end of the day, then he would tell his kind, generous, warmhearted wonderful family that now he, Francisco, was an employed person and presently could get his own room somewhere so that the boys would not have to go on sleeping with their feet in each other's face.

Only then would he tell.

At dinner Mrs. Orgella said to Simone, "Did you see Franny, *querida mía?*"

"No," Simone began, "I—"

"Boys!" Mrs. Orgella interrupted. "Stop that! Any more fooling around that way and I'll send you straight from the table!"

"*He* did it," said one of the brothers. "He kicked me under the table!"

"He's a liar. I didn't kick him. I was trying to find my shoe, it fell off—"

Franny was out of the conversation as the tempestuous Orgella family made its way through dinner. The boys had, at length, to be sent protesting furiously from the table. José screamed for chili, settled angrily for zwieback. Mr. Orgella threatened to leave home if everybody didn't please shut up.

Grandmother Orgella told her daughter-in-law that she couldn't cook to please a swine. . . .

Under the racket Simone said anxiously to Francisco, "Francisco, do you think somebody with *quality* would betray somebody else? I mean, a friend?"

"Absolutely not," Francisco said promptly. "Not a friend or an enemy, I should say. Betray them how?"

"Oh, tell a secret."

"No," said Francisco. "I do not for one minute believe that such a thing could happen."

Slightly comforted, Simone fell silent, and Francisco, absorbed with his own thoughts, did not pursue the matter as he ordinarily might have. He ate steadily and dreamed, with alternate delight and apprehension, of tomorrow's destiny.

After dinner everybody became friendly again as a matter of course, since no one, except possibly Grandmother Orgella, had really been angry to begin with. The Orgellas were simply a big family with large emotions trying to contain them in a small apartment.

Chapter Eleven

According to the current-events teacher, there were more than eight million people living in New York City. Franny thought of them all, squashed together in apartment buildings, crowding into buses, hurrying down subway steps, riding up and down in elevators, spreading out in all the offices and restaurants, and sitting around Washington Square.

Eight million of them.

Some of those people had a lot of money, and some, she suspected, were even poorer than the Davises. Franny had seen old men on winter nights huddled in doorways, sleeping. If you had to sleep in a doorway, if you had nowhere to go out of the night and the bitter cold, you were as poor, she guessed, as you could be. By comparison the Davises were rich. Probably.

But of all the eight million, Franny somehow felt during the following week that none of them had more troubles than she had. Did anyone else have a father who couldn't get a job, a house to come home to where just about nobody talked anymore, a friend who hadn't said a word to her for days, and a little brother who wasn't going to have a birthday at all when Friday came?

Nothing seemed to help.

Miss Rose picked a painting of Franny's and hung it in her art room class, saying it was the best picture any pupil of hers had done all year. Instead of making Franny happy, that worsened matters because Simone, who adored Miss Rose, got even friendlier with Lila Wembleton after the picture went up.

Jealous, Franny said to herself. Just jealous. She was right, and it didn't help at all. She watched Simone and Lila giggle together and whisper at lunchtime and during recess. Once when their eyes met, Simone hesitated and then made a gesture of invitation toward Franny. Or *maybe* it was of invitation.

Franny was too proud to join them and find out. Suppose she should walk over and find that that wasn't what Simone had meant at all? She turned away, lonely in the way that only losing a friend can make a person lonely.

And she didn't, she found, really have anyone to talk to about it. Marshall was a darling, but only a baby. She certainly couldn't talk to Jim, who wouldn't have listened anyway. Jim had so many friends that he probably wouldn't notice for weeks if he lost one. Her parents—well, they were like two sad shadows. Sometimes she could talk to them. Sometimes they were the best of all to talk to. But since Papa had lost his job they hadn't seemed to want to talk at all, to anyone, about anything.

No, the only person she could have talked to about this was the person who was causing it, and this gave Franny the greatest unhappiness of all.

One thing afforded her pleasure during these days. It was the birthday present she was making for Marshall. She worked on it during study hour, during recess, and right after lunch. At least it kept her from having to watch Lila and Simone giggling together. And even if nobody else remembered or was going to do anything about it, *she* was going to have a present ready for Marshall on his birthday. She had tried to ask her mother and father if they could have a party, even a little one, but Mama had started to cry and Papa had put the newspaper in front of his face.

Today after she left school she wandered down the street by herself, more slowly than usual, even though she knew Marshall would be waiting at the head of the stairs, legs twined around the banister, looking forward to the tray school.

"Hey, Franny! *Psst!*"

She turned in surprise, then saw that she was outside the shoe store where her father had worked. There was Francisco in the doorway, looking pleased. And there, in the window, sure enough, was the oil painting her father had done of Mr. Horney. Underneath it was a nice card lettered *Samuel Eggerston Horney, Founder.* In smaller but still distinct letters it said, *Artist, Mr. James W. Davis, A.U.A.*

Franny was impressed. She walked over to Francisco, and they stood together admiring the sign.

"What does A.U.A. mean?" Franny asked.

"Academy of Unrecognized Artists," Francisco explained. "Tulio likes a few initials after a painter's name. He says it gives tone."

"It certainly does," Franny agreed, transferring her attention to the painting.

"It's got this greenish look," she said at length. "I like it, but it's greenish."

"Mr. Horney," Francisco said firmly, "is a noted woodsman. By this fine painter's device your father has shown the essential character of his subject."

"I see," said Franny.

"Your father is one very fine painter."

"I know."

"One day the world will know it."

"I hope so. I wish he'd get a job in between. Do you like it here, Francisco?"

"I love it," Francisco said earnestly. "I love the leather and the customers and the shape of the shoes and Mr. Horney, who worries all the time and is such a nice man."

"Is he really a woodsman, Francisco?"

Francisco laughed and wouldn't answer.

"I guess you're a good shoe salesman," Franny went on.

"I begin to believe it is true. I have waited. I have not told a member of my lovely family that at last I am an employed person. They think I'm still out every day looking for a job. But I wanted to be sure, you know?"

"Oh, yes," said Franny. She knew the feeling of not wanting to say a thing out loud for fear mere spoken words would cause it not to be so.

All at once there was something she did want to say to Francisco, and she put it into words quickly, before she could change her mind. "Francisco, do you know why Simone doesn't talk to me anymore?"

If she'd given herself time to think, she would not have spoken. Pride would have risen to stop her. But she knew, the way she sometimes did just *know* things, that here, when she'd thought there was nobody, here was a person she could talk to.

"Ah," said Francisco thoughtfully. "I feared this. She is friendly just now with that poor little girl Lila, no?"

"Yes. Except she isn't a poor little girl. At least I don't think so. Her father owns the whole building they live in. All the stoves and the stairways and the doors and everything. It all belongs to him." The concept was overwhelming to Franny, who kept trying not to be impressed by the thought of somebody's owning a whole apartment building and went right on being impressed.

"Well, I wasn't thinking so much of that," said Francisco. "I was thinking of the poor little Lila herself, who never seems to keep a friend."

Franny deliberated. That was true enough. Lila changed friends all the time, and the truth was that nobody really liked her very much, in spite of her dancing lessons and her lunch box and her fancy room that Franny had never seen.

"I don't seem to keep one either," she said dully. "Friend, I mean."

"You are a different case altogether. You have to do so much work at home, which doesn't leave you much time for forming a great many friendships. Besides," Francisco went on, "the important thing is to have good friends, not lots of friends."

"But I don't have either!" Franny burst out.

"You and Simone argued over something? Said harsh things to each other?"

"I don't know," Franny said miserably. "I guess so. We had sort of an argument about—about the scabs on my knees." That sounded so silly that she added quickly, "There was something else, but I don't remember. The thing about Simone," she went on passionately, "is she wants everything to be beautiful all the time. Well, everything *isn't* beautiful all the time. Some things aren't beautiful any of the time, and scabs aren't. But they're *there,* and people *get* them, and what are you supposed to do, throw yourself down a well while they go away? And besides, how about how *she* doesn't put down the curtain in front of the kitchen? I don't think *that's* so very beautiful, let me tell you. Leaving a kitchen right out there in the open with the dirty dishes and all when you don't have to." She stopped, out of breath.

Francisco leaned against the shoe store door. "You know what it takes to make a friendship? A real friendship?"

Franny sniffled. At length, because he didn't go on, she said curiously, "Well, what?"

"Compromise. You know what that is?"

"Not really."

"Compromise is when you say, 'This is a person I am truly fond of, and he'—or she, you understand— 'has some ways that I am not fond of at all. But because my fondness is so great, I will overlook these things. Because the whole person is more important to me than these little pieces I do not care for, I will overlook them. Because friendship is more important than anything else, I will overlook them.' "

"Why doesn't Simone overlook my knees?"

"Why don't you see that it doesn't matter if she leaves the kitchen uncurtained?"

"It *doesn't* matter to me," Franny explained. "It's just that she talks all the *time* about *beauty*. I mean, if you're going to talk about it that much, why don't you do something about it?"

"In that apartment?" Francisco let out a long breath. "Some people live so crowded, so without a decent space around them to breathe in, that they lose hope. Simone, I think, dreams of when everything around her will be fragrant and furry and silken. But she can't see how to find it where she is. She's afraid she may never find it. That's why she cuts out pictures but doesn't bother about the curtain. Why do you cut out pictures?"

"I like to see other lands and animals and colors."

"Your dreams, some of them, are in your scrapbook. I think all of Simone's are. Forget about the curtain in front of the kitchen, Franny."

"*I'm* willing to forget it," Franny said indignantly. "It's Simone who isn't talking to me, remember?"

"Why don't you go to her and say, 'Simone, my friend, whatever it was, and I don't remember what it was, let us forget it.' "

But Franny couldn't do that, and if he couldn't see how she couldn't, there was no point in talking further. She bid him farewell and walked on. Even if you could talk to Francisco, you couldn't get any help from him. She wondered if that was the way it was all the time, with everybody, if that was the way it would always be.

It was such a depressing idea that by the time she got home she couldn't run up the stairs to Marshall. She trudged, pulling herself along by the railing. Marshall, under the skylight, waiting, frowned when he saw her. He was being made very nervous this week. He didn't know why he felt the way he felt, but he'd been so bad today that Mrs. Mundy had had to scold him four times.

"Why is your face that way?" he demanded as Franny arrived at the landing.

"What way?"

"Cross. And *mean*," he exaggerated. "Everybody's mean to me today."

"Oh, Marshall, be quiet," Franny said. "I'm not mean, and I'll thank you to leave me alone."

Marshall dissolved into howling tears, and even when Franny hugged him and said she hadn't really meant it, even when they got out the tray school (Franny had forgotten to get it ready in the morning) and did geography, he kept having this feeling that he was going to be bad again and scolded again, and he didn't know why. He didn't know why at all.

Every morning Mr. Davis left right after breakfast.

Every evening when he came in, his wife and children looked up quickly to read a job in his face and looked away again when they saw nothing. Jimmy got sent to the principal's office twice, the first time for alarming a substitute teacher with his tales about giant rats in the basement, and the second time for not going when he was sent the first time. Then one evening Mrs. Mundy came across the hall to announce that Marshall was behaving like a hooligan lately.

"And I don't know, I'm sure," she went on, refusing to sit down, "whether I shall be able to go on taking care of him if this keeps up."

Marshall, squeezing Fudge against his chest, glared at her. He opened his mouth to say it would be fine with him if she didn't ever take care of him again, but Franny seemed to know what he had in mind and practically sat on his head to keep him from talking. By the time Fudge had yowled and fled and Marshall had gotten free of his sister, his chance to speak was past.

"So please, if you'll just understand and forgive him," Mrs. Davis was saying, "I am sure Marshall won't give you any more trouble. Will you, Marshall?" she said fixing him with an icy eye.

Marshall returned his mother's gaze, then looked at his father, his sister, and even at Jimmy. He pondered. Now, if he could, there was a chance for him to tell Mrs. Mundy he didn't want to stay in her old apartment anyway. He could say, "Oh, go fish, Mrs. Mundy." Once again he looked at Franny, at his father, at his mother.

"No," he said.

"No what, Marshall?" said Mrs. Davis. "We don't understand what you mean by 'no.'" He remained silent, and she went on, "Mrs. Mundy and your father and I are waiting, Marshall."

"I mean"—Marshall dragged the words out—"I mean I won't behave like a hool . . . like that no more."

"Anymore," said Franny.

Marshall nodded. "Anymore," he muttered.

"Well," said Mrs. Mundy. "Well, I don't know, I'm sure. Well, we'll try again, won't we, Marshall?"

He nodded, and after Mrs. Mundy was gone he went into the bedroom and played with his toy cars on the windowsill. Even when one of them accidentally fell out and down to the alley below in all the trash where he would never be able to find it again, he didn't go back to his family. He waited and waited for Franny to come in and tell him everything was all right. But she didn't. Tears fell down his cheeks, and Fudge nestled against him without purring.

In the living room Jim and Franny did their homework. Mr. Davis sat in the big chair with his eyes closed, thinking. Mrs. Davis turned the collars of some shirts.

Won't be a problem pretty soon anyway, thought

Mr. Davis. I'll have to start taking Marsh around with me to employment agencies, because after next week I won't be able to pay Mrs. Mundy even the little bit we pay her for looking after him. And that, in turn, was going to be hard on Mrs. Mundy, who barely kept body and soul together as it was and was too old to go out and get a regular job.

What a mess we're all in, he thought. What a mess the world is in. Wars and strife and poverty and hatred and misunderstanding. He opened his eyes and looked at his son, at his daughter. His heart was so full of love for them that it seemed to press against his chest.

"You know," Jim said suddenly, "the old bat could *cut* those four hairs off her chin, couldn't she?"

Mr. Davis jumped to his feet. "You unkind, disrespectful whelp, I ought to take you over my knee for that."

Jim looked up in amazement. "Over your *knee?*" he said. "How old do you think I am? This is Jim, you know. Not Marshall."

"Don't you talk to me like that," Mr. Davis shouted, taking a step forward. "We'll have some respect around here, do you understand?"

Jim, under most circumstances, would have replied to anyone who spoke to him like that, "Respect for what?" But he didn't say it. He said nothing at all, and after a while Mr. Davis turned wearily away. Mrs. Davis put her fingers on her forehead. Franny studied a map of Alaska with blurred vision.

"I'm sorry," said Jim, surprising them all. "I'm sorry, Papa."

Franny wondered what Nome was like and wished she were there to see, and didn't look up from her book. But Jim's words helped in some fashion. As if he'd stopped a storm that had been approaching, that had been going to sweep like a torrent over them, leaving them stranded and separated like people in newsreel floods.

But it was strange, she said to herself, how when things got so terrible at home, you didn't even care what was going on someplace else. For the past couple of days it hadn't seemed to matter that Simone and Lila were together so much. At lunchtime today Simone had definitely waved to her, and Franny had only realized it after she'd taken a seat someplace else. By then it was too late to get up and change. Or anyway she'd decided it was too late.

She wondered suddenly if Francisco still had his job and if he still liked it. By the end of the week, by Friday—Marshall's birthday—if he still had it he was going to tell the Orgellas. But it was funny, her father getting Simone's cousin a job, and still Simone wasn't talking to her.

"How does Francisco like his job?" she said, determined to put an end to the silence in this room.

"Well, now," said Mr. Davis heartily. "I don't know. Seeing as he's my protégé, in a sense, I should drop around and see. Tomorrow after my—my rounds I'll do it. It would be a nice thing to do, don't you think?"

"Yes, Papa," she said, smiling at him. "I think he'd like it very much."

She got up and went in to see what Marshall was doing.

The following evening, Thursday, Mr. Davis came home looking brighter, but he held up his hand and said quickly, "No, I didn't get one. Although I have a couple of excellent prospects. Excellent." They all attempted to look as if this might well be so and waited to see why he was cheerful at all. "I have," he went on, "an invitation from Mr. Horney for all of us to stop by the store and be fitted for shoes this evening."

"Papa!" said Franny. "Oh, that's dreamy. Mama, can I get patent leather, *please?*"

"You will get sturdy school shoes, dear," said Mrs. Davis, still looking at her husband. "How—what's the reason after all this time?"

"Well, now, my dear. It's all because of that confounded portrait I did. Would you believe it, business has picked up since he put it in the window? Mr. Horney doesn't seem to recall that he put it in at the same time that he hired Francisco, and it is my personal opinion that Francisco, not my art, is responsible for the commercial spurt in Horney's line. Still I don't like to point this out until we actually get the shoes."

"You're sure we don't have to pay for them?" Mrs. Davis said.

He shook his head. "Not a cent. Mr. Horney is giving us each a pair of shoes in exchange for the portrait."

"Well, then, Papa," said Franny, "you've sold a picture, haven't you? Like Tulio? You've bartered it, the way they did in Colonial days."

"You are right, you are perfectly right," said Mr. Davis happily. "So now let us hie ourselves to the bootery, citizens!"

On the way downstairs Mrs. Davis said in a low voice, "Couldn't we have saved the shoes for tomorrow and given them to Marshall for his birthday?"

His bright mood ebbing, Mr. Davis firmly shook his head.

"Children should not get something they *need* for a present. Besides, what sort of present would Marshall think it was with everybody else getting the same thing? Can we make him the cake?" She nodded. "And we have candles?" She nodded again.

Mr. Davis said fine, that was fine. But it was with a good deal of difficulty that he recaptured part of his earlier good spirits. Even in the shoe store, with Mr. Horney himself waiting on them and explaining to everybody what a fine artist they had for a papa, even then Mr. Davis went on thinking about Marshall's birthday and what to do about it.

Chapter Twelve

And then when his birthday did arrive, Marshall forgot it.

Spending the day as usual with Mrs. Mundy, he noticed that she was especially nice to him, but he figured that was maybe because it was Friday. Mrs. Mundy was always cheery on Friday, because after it came Saturday and Sunday, when she didn't have to take care of him. Or maybe she was just being nice because some of the time she was. Only usually it didn't last all day.

They went to the market together, where she let him dawdle as much as he wanted to. She didn't even hold his hand except when they were crossing the street. She let him turn on the television himself and look at one of the programs he wasn't supposed to look at where everybody killed everybody else. After a while he turned it off. She let him bring Fudge across the hall to her apartment, which had never been done before. Fudge could only stay long enough for lunch—he had evaporated milk and a spoonful of the tuna fish Mrs. Mundy was fixing for her lunch and Marshall's—and then he had to go right back. But it was pretty nice of her to invite him at all, Marshall thought.

Still he waited eagerly for the big hand to be at twelve and the little hand to be at three. Every day it was good when Franny came home, but Fridays were especially wonderful because of Saturday and Sunday coming next.

Promptly at three he bid Mrs. Mundy good-bye, thanked her for the nice day, and went out to the top of the stairs. Sunshine came through the dusty skylight, brightening the hallway somewhat, and in just a couple of minutes Franny came running up the stairs, red sweater flying, hair flopping.

"Well," she asked when she'd put her books away and admired her new shoes for a little before she took them off and got into her old ones, "shall we work first or play first?"

"Work," said Marshall, thinking to surprise her.

Franny's face fell. "For goodness' sake, Marsh. What do you mean? We always play first."

"Yes, but I thought today we could change around. For a change. I'll help you set the table and peel something and then we'll play school."

"Why change today?" she asked, looking upset. "No. I'm the teacher, and I say we play first."

"You aren't the teacher until we start playing," he pointed out.

"Marshall, don't be difficult," she said sternly, and then, "What are you smiling at?"

"You sound just like Papa. *Marshall don't be difficult,*" he echoed. "That's just the way Papa says it."

"Are we going to play school or aren't we?"

"Oh, sure, Franny."

"Then please go to your desk, pupil."

They did geography, and Marshall, who had always wanted to learn where Philadelphia was, learned. It was in Pennsylvania. He picked it out on the map in Franny's schoolbook. He could also pick out New York and New Jersey and Connecticut, but started to go to pieces when they got to Massachusetts.

"That's all right," Franny consoled him. "Most boys your age never even heard of Massachusetts."

"Really?" said Marshall with pleasure. "What about if they live there?" he added.

Franny smiled at him. "You know, Marsh, I think you're going to grow up to be very smart."

"You do?" he said, more and more pleased.

"I do. And that'll be even better than being rich."

Marshall didn't know about that, but he didn't have time to argue because Franny said school was now over for the day, and she wouldn't let him come in the kitchen to help with dinner preparations.

"Not tonight," she said. "In fact, I am going to close the kitchen door, and you aren't to come in."

"Why? Why can't I help?"

"Because," she explained firmly.

"Oh. Oh, all right. What shall I do?"

"I am going to give you some homework, and you must sit at your desk and do it."

This was very much to Marshall's taste, since he had never had any homework to do before.

Franny went into the kitchen, closing the door behind her, and left Marshall sitting at the tray school, practicing his *K*'s. He still refused to study *J*'s properly and wouldn't write them down at all.

Mr. and Mrs. Davis came home. Mrs. Davis went into the kitchen with Franny and the door went on being closed. Jim came in early. And still Marshall didn't remember what day this was. He showed Papa his *K*'s and some numbers he'd put in for fun.

"Homework, eh?" said Mr. Davis. "Well, that shows you're making progress."

Jim started to snort, then coughed instead, and

after that Papa read to Marshall out of the newspaper about "New Residents at the Zoo" (a llama and a rare gray seal), and "Commuters Delayed Up to Three Hours, Owing to Balky Steam Hose Connection." He was explaining what a balky steam hose connection was when Marshall's birthday began.

It came in a splendid rushing surprise, with even Mrs. Mundy arriving from across the hall, carrying a package, and all of them—Papa, Mama, Franny, Jim, and Mrs. Mundy—standing in a row, singing, "Happy Birthday to you, Happy Birthday to you, Happy Birthday, dear Marshall, Happy Birthday to you."

Marshall gasped as the full significance of the event dawned on him. His birthday! His actual very own birthday had come at last. Just for a moment he was vexed that all day he hadn't remembered and that all day no one had reminded him.

But how could anyone continue to be vexed when all this singing was going on just for him? When under Mrs. Mundy's arm was that wrapped-up package, and another in Franny's hand, and still another in Papa's? Mrs. Mundy's was the biggest, Papa's the smallest, but only Jimmy had nothing at all. Mama was holding Fudge and a can of sardines tied with a red ribbon.

When they'd stopped singing, Mrs. Davis said, "Fudge asked me to give you this and explain that he's feeling a bit hoarse tonight or he'd wish you a happy birthday himself."

Marshall smiled. He was especially fond of sardines. So was Fudge. "Thank you, Fudge," he said seriously.

"Tell him it's just what you wanted," Franny urged, and Fudge took that moment to meow, so they all laughed.

Then they went in to dinner, and Marshall saw now why the door had been closed against him. On the kitchen table was the paper birthday tablecloth that Mama had bought for Franny and Jim's birthday in April. It looked as good as new, just about, with dishes carefully covering the spots. The corner that Fudge had chewed had been trimmed into a design with scissors, and the other corners trimmed to match. It looked wonderful. And somewhere in the kitchen, Marshall knew, there was a cake. It was hidden from view, *but it was there*. He tried not to look around, in case they hadn't hidden it enough.

They had hot dogs, which Marshall was especially fond of, and mashed potatoes and jellied salad. He was especially fond of all these too.

And then—oh, then came the cake, out from the dish closet, where it had been hiding.

It was a cake of great beauty. Chocolate. Chocolate on top, chocolate underneath, chocolate in between. And in curly yellow icing writing it said *Happy Birthday, Marshall* all across the top. Six yellow candles fluttered their flames like tiny flags, five for his years, and one to grow on. Everybody sang again while Marshall was persuaded to blow them out.

He did not want to blow the candles out but finally did, and six little streamers of smoke rose in the air, with the special candly smell he remembered from Franny and Jimmy's birthday. He was glad to be having one all for himself tonight. Sometimes he wanted to be a twin like them, but not on his birthday.

When the cake had been eaten, the part about the presents arrived.

Marshall tried not to stare first at Mrs. Mundy's, but it looked so packagy and so much bigger than the others that he had a hard time.

"Why don't you open that one first?" said Papa. "As our guest brought it, that would seem only right."

Marshall sighed and said, all right, he would. He took the bright ribbon off with care. It was green with gold dots on it. Carefully he began to peel away the Scotch tape from the wrapping. It was green and red and sort of left over from Christmas. Jim wriggled in his chair, but Marshall went on taking his time. He liked to make a present last.

And then—the moment of revelation.

"Oh, *my!*" said Franny. "*Oh, my . . .*"

"How marvelous!" said Mama.

"How clever!" said Papa.

Mrs. Mundy beamed at everybody and said nothing.

Jim, who'd begun by being amused at Marshall's idea of a party—the family and an old neighbor from across the hall—was by now annoyed all around, even a little bit at himself, because he was the only one without a present. He said nothing as he stared at Mrs. Mundy's present, but his eyes widened.

For Mrs. Mundy had given Marshall a whole big boxful of cereal surprises.

"Acres of them," breathed Marshall in a daze. "Just *acres*."

There were Chinese puzzles, bird cards, little plastic spacemen with helmets and uniforms on, little plastic automobiles, little plastic soldiers and trucks and animals, baseball cards, three balloons with cat faces stamped on them, a spoon with the Empire State Building stamped in the bowl, football cards, Egyptian puzzles, two FASCINATING word games, and a plastic ocarina.

"Boy, you sure must eat a heck of a lot of cereal," Jim muttered, then quailed under his father's eye. "I'm sorry, Mrs. Mundy," he said quickly. "I didn't mean anything."

"I have saved my cereal surprises for some time," she informed him loftily. "I have also had my sisters, Emma and Sue Virginia, saving their cereal surprises. In this manner the surprises have mounted up quite—ah—surprisingly." She turned to Marshall again, her face expectant.

"Oh, it's *just* what I wanted," he breathed, and everyone looked gratified. Everyone except Jim, who tried to look gratified but couldn't.

"And now mine," said Franny. "Open mine, darling Marshall."

Exercising the same degree of care, Marshall made his way into his sister's present. It had blue ribbon and was wrapped in blue and silver paper that had wedding bells printed on it. Franny explained that Miss Rose had given it to her, that it was from a present that Miss Rose's sister had gotten.

"She got married," Franny said, not taking her eyes from Marshall. "The sister, I mean."

"How could we ever of guessed," said Jimmy. Nobody paid any attention to him.

Marshall laid back the last fold of paper and there the present was. A book. A book Franny had made herself. It had the alphabet on all the right-hand pages and numbers on all the left-hand pages and a whole entire map of the United States of America on the cover. She had crayoned the numbers and the letters and all the states with different-colored crayons, and fastened the pages together with staples and a manly looking leather shoelace.

"Oh, *Franny*," said Marshall. "Oh Franny. It's the beautifulest book I ever *saw*."

"Are you sure?" she said anxiously.

"Oh, yes. I'm very sure."

"Well," said Mr. Davis, "I'm sure it's the beauti-fulest—I mean, the most beautiful book that anyone ever got."

"And the nicest," said Mrs. Davis.

"And the most thoughtful," said Mrs. Mundy.

Suddenly Jim jumped to his feet. He walked around to his brother and bent his head down. "Bop me," he said.

"Huh?" said Marshall.

"Bop me, I said. G'wan . . . go ahead and bop me."

"Jimmy, what are you talking about?" said Mrs. Davis.

Jim straightened. "I didn't get him a present, so I figure for my present I'll just let him bop me. He's always wanting to, so I figure it'd be a pretty good present, letting him." He leaned over again. "Go ahead, Marsh, bop. Hard as you want. I'm wait-ing."

"*What* a peculiar present," said Mrs. Mundy, get-ting back at Jim. "Definitely odd."

Marshall lifted his hand over Jim's head, clenched his fist, scowled, hesitated, looked at the others, who said nothing. Well, this was a chance he'd never have again, or anyway not until he was grown up, so he'd better go ahead and bop.

But he opened his fist and patted his brother's head and decided to tell Franny that after all he'd study his *J*'s.

"Oh, but gosh," said Jim, rather pleased by the

gentle pat, but still left in the position of having given nothing. "Gee whiz, I'm the only one that didn't."

"I suppose we could say that at least you tried," said Mr. Davis. "But I'm not sure I want to say it." Privately he agreed with Mrs. Mundy that it was a most peculiar present.

And now Marshall's eyes moved to the last present, a slim, flat thing wrapped in red tissue paper with a tag dangling from it.

"That's from you and Mama," he said.

Mr. Davis looked at the tag. "So it is, so it is. Is it your pleasure to open it now?"

"So it is," said Marshall, laughing. "So it is."

He studied the tag, which had printing on it, and he recognized some of his letters. *A*'s for instance. There were a lot of *A*'s. And that was an *F*. He scanned the tag carefully, looking for familiar faces.

"What are you doing, Marsh?" Jim said impatiently.

"Reading my card." Marshall continued to pore over the letters. An *E*, that was. But he couldn't seem to find—

"Reading, eh?" said Jim heartily. "Well, that's pretty smart of you. But couldn't you read a little faster?"

Marshall looked up. "On your birthday, you can go as fast as you want, Jimmy. And on my birthday, I can go as slow as I want. See?" He returned to the problem, found nothing else to recognize, and decided to let Franny read the rest of his tag for him.

"Love to Marshall, from Mama and Papa," she read.

Marshall smiled. "That's what I knew it said."

He proceeded to the opening. Inside the red tissue was a yellow envelope, and inside the yellow envelope was something wrapped in white tissue, and inside the white tissue he found one sheet of paper and one white cardboard—

He glanced up doubtfully. White cardboard what?

"That's a ticket," said Franny with a squeal of recognition. "It's a ticket, isn't it, Papa?"

Mr. Davis nodded.

"Where's it to, Marshall?" Franny went on, leaning closer to look.

"Yes," said Marshall. "Where's it to?"

He examined the ticket curiously. There was handsome black lettering printed on it (Tulio's work) and on the sheet of paper there was some typewriting. But he was so anxious to discover his destination that he didn't take time to read the part he could read. He simply thrust the whole present at his sister.

"*You* see," he told her.

"Well, now," she murmured. "Now this one—the ticket—it says ONE WAY, FRIDAY EVENING TO SATUR-DAY MORNING."

Marshall blinked and looked at his parents. He

wasn't quite sure what it meant, but he was almost sure. "What does the paper say, Franny? Hurry up."

"It says, *Davis Travel Bureau, Itinerary for Marshall Davis.* That's at the top. Then it says, *Tour includes walk in Greenwich Village streets and avenues after bedtime. Also two guides for term of ticket. Reasonable requests granted. Bearer entitled to 15¢ worth of refreshments.*"

"Papa! Mama!" Marshall shouted. "I'm not going to bed tonight, am I?"

"You mean we're going to stay up all night?" Jimmy asked.

"Not you, dear," said his mother. Jim's jaw dropped. "It isn't your birthday," she explained.

"You mean Franny and I have to go to bed and he doesn't?"

Mr. Davis started to frown, then looked carefully at Jim and smiled slightly. Jim, it appeared, was continuing to practice his peculiar version of birthday giving. This notion seemed more successful than his earlier one, because Marshall was looking smugly pleased. *He* was to watch *them* go to bed, like babies, while he remained with the grown-ups and even went out in the night.

After a while, when Mrs. Mundy had heard again how much Marshall like her marvelous and surprising surprise, she took her leave, and as she was going out the door a commotion in the hallway announced that others were coming.

"Company!" said Marshall. "Company's coming for the party!"

Exchanging glances, Mr. and Mrs. Davis went to the door, where Mr. Horney and Francisco were standing together, both talking at once.

". . . all because of Francisco here, and a finer salesman I have never met, you should excuse the expression, Davis, but when all's said and done you weren't the best—"

". . . nothing to do with me at all," Francisco was protesting. "Simply and purely a matter of great good fortune and Providence smiling on us so that Mr. Wheeler came down that block and not down some other block, *madre mía,* think if he'd decided to walk on West *Fifteenth,* or Thirteenth—or anyway not *Fourteenth . . ."*

"What is it all about?" Mr. Davis said when he'd got the two of them seated but couldn't stop their tongues. "Who is Mr. Wheeler?"

" 'Who is Mr. Wheeler,' he says." Mr. Horney looked at Francisco and laughed. "He says 'Who is Mr. Wheeler.' "

"Well, who is Mr. Wheeler?" said Jim.

"*He* says it too," exclaimed Mr. Horney, throwing his arms in the air. " 'Who is Mr. Wheeler.' He says it too."

Francisco rubbed his nose. "In fact, señor," he pointed out, "they do not know who Mr. Wheeler is. I am afraid we haven't told them."

"Haven't told them?" said Mr. Horney. "What are we here for if not to talk about Mr. Wheeler?"

"Aren't you here for my birthday?" said Marshall.

"Well," said Mr. Davis, laughing. "We're very happy to have you, for whatever reason. And it is our son Marshall's birthday, you'll be happy to know."

"I'm five," Marshall explained. "Going on six."

"Well, well, well," said Mr. Horney. "Congratulations, young fellow. Think of it. Five years old. Did you have a party?"

"Yes," said Marshall. "And *lots* of presents."

"That's the way it should be," Mr. Horney approved. "A person's birthday should not go unobserved." His face fell briefly, as his own birthday always went unobserved. Then he brightened. "At your age they shouldn't, anyway. When one gets older, it doesn't seem to matter so much."

Marshall doubted that, but then the conversation left the interesting topic of him and his age and went back to Mr. Wheeler, so Marshall lost interest. He began to think about the night, the entire whole night until morning, that was stretching before him. He was the *only person here* with a printed ticket to tomorrow morning.

"Mr. Hubert Wheeler," Mr. Horney said to the others. "A patron of the arts."

"Oh?" said Mr. Davis tensely. "Indeed?" No one else spoke as they waited for Mr. Horney to.

"A patron of the arts, you understand. So naturally

when he passed my shoe store he could not help being struck by your fine painting. He stopped out there looking for so long that Francisco and I were sure we had a sale. Those genuine imitation English brogans next to your picture, we thought. So when at last he did step in, I advanced and said 'How do you do, sir. May I show you something in the way of a brogan?' I thought I would handle the sale myself to show Francisco how an important sale should be made."

Francisco nodded. "Beautifully done," he said. "It was beautifully approached."

"Only he didn't want any shoes." Mr. Horney was coming to the climax of his story. He sat back in the big chair and stared at his audience. "No, he wanted no shoes."

"What did he want?" Franny breathed.

"You may well ask," said Mr. Horney, sitting straight again. "You may well ask."

"Yeah, but may you well answer?" Jimmy muttered.

Fortunately Mr. Horney was too absorbed to hear. "He had come in, this Mr. Hubert Wheeler, for the express purpose of inquiring"—his voice grew low and thrilling—" of inquiring, *'Who is the painter of that picture in the window?'* "

There was a pause while everyone let out his breath.

"Yes," said Mr. Horney, sitting back once again.

"That is what he asked. And I replied, 'The artist is Mr. James W. Davis, of this city.' 'And what,' Mr. Wheeler went on, 'does A.U.A. stand for?' "

Mr. Davis caught his lip with his teeth and exchanged a glance with Francisco. "I said to him, 'Mr. Wheeler, in all honesty, I cannot tell you. The sign painter put those initials after Mr. Davis's name and I questioned them not. A few initials after a painter's name is not so uncommon.' By the way"—he looked at Mr. Davis—"what do they stand for?"

"Oh"—Mr. Davis waved his hands—"a small society. One Tulio and I belong to. Perfectly bona fide, you understand, but I think we'd better stop calling attention to it."

"Ah. Well, in any case, Mr. Wheeler didn't seem interested in that. He said he'd like to meet you, so Francisco and I volunteered to stop by this evening and ask you kindly to call on him—here, here is the address. He wants to see more of your paintings."

"See my paintings?" Mr. Davis breathed. "He wants to look at my paintings? Why I—I— But this is hard to believe."

"Nevertheless," said Mr. Horney, "this is the simple fact of the matter. He wishes to see more of your work. That was how he put it. 'I wish to see more of this man's work,' he said."

Mr. Davis put a hand on his forehead, a gesture of his when baffled, and Mrs. Davis reached over to take his other hand.

167 ✄

"Mr. Horney," she said, "who *is* Mr. Wheeler? I mean, you seem to be saying somehow that he is more than—than a person casually interested in looking at paintings. Is he? Are you saying that?"

Mr. Horney got to his feet, and with an air triumphant and dramatic, said, "He owns an art gallery on Fifty-seventh Street." In the stunned silence that followed, he added, "Now, may I be permitted to contribute to the birthday celebration? Some ice cream? Some Italian ice? A few sparklers if we can find them?"

Being told by a dazed Mrs. Davis that that would be perfectly lovely of him, he went off with Jimmy to see what they could find.

Mrs. Davis began to clear the dishes from the table, and Mr. Davis followed her into the kitchen.

"It's so hard to believe," he said again. "A dealer. A gallery. He wants to see my paintings. It's so *hard* to believe."

"I know. Why is it that often good news seems more unbelievable than bad?" Mrs. Davis was attempting to be casual, unelated. She was trying not to look directly at this dazzling development for fear a too close scrutiny would cause it to flicker and go out.

"To think," he said, shaking his head in wonder, "that if I hadn't given Mr. Horney the painting—" He broke off, resumed in a brisker tone. "This may be an omen, you see. This may be the turning point for us."

Mrs. Davis stopped trying to be casual. She said proudly, "It may, oh, it may. Something wonderful must come of this."

They looked at each other with that rising hope that human beings, no matter what the past has been, can always bring to fresh occasions.

Meanwhile Marshall in the living room was simply gloating. He regarded his box of cereal surprises; turned the pages of his own book, made for him, with the beautiful colors; and studied his ticket from to-night to tomorrow morning. Franny and Jimmy would have to go to bed pretty soon, but he would not. He was going to stay up all night and do any-thing he wanted to. His hand hovered over Mrs. Mundy's box, his eyes were shining, his mind was a kaleidoscope of pleasures and plans.

"What a pleasant sight is a perfectly happy per-son," said Francisco.

Franny nodded, but she was thinking more of her parents than of Marshall. It seemed such a long time since she had seen them looking the way they did now. As if—she remembered her mother's words of the other day—as if they had a lot to live for. She sighed happily, wriggled a little on the sofa next to Francisco, and wondered all at once what Simone was doing.

Chapter Thirteen

Marshall stood in the middle of the living room and looked slowly around. Nighttime was very different from daytime. He had always known this would be so. This was how it was in here when Papa and Mama were alone, when he and Franny and Jimmy had gone to bed. Fudge was still here. He didn't usually come into the bedroom until later.

It was so quiet.

"What do you do after we go to bed?" he asked his

father. Mr. Davis, happy and bewildered, was sitting in his big chair, thinking about his meeting with Mr. Wheeler.

"Do?" he said after a moment. "About what?"

"You must do something," Marshall insisted. "You don't just sit."

"I love just sitting."

"Sometimes I cook," said Mrs. Davis. "So as to be ahead."

"I know," said Marshall. "I can smell it sometimes. Stew, and like that. What else do you do?"

"We read," Mr. Davis offered. "And talk. Your mother and I like to talk."

"About what?"

"Politics and kings. Love and money. You children."

"What else do you do?"

"Let's see. Your mother sews a great deal. It seems to me that one day we may end up wearing just the threads that once held the cloth together."

Marshall laughed at this and then asked what else they did.

"Oh, nights when Mrs. Mundy comes over to sit with you children, we visit friends or take a walk. Once in a while we go to a movie."

"What else?"

"That's about it, I'd say."

"It is?" said Marshall. "But you're all grown up. You could do anything."

"For instance, what?"

Marshall tried to think of all the things he and Franny planned to do when they were finally grown up and free to do everything they wanted.

Mermaids, presidents, firemen, rich . . . he realized that somehow none of these ideas quite fitted in with Mama and Papa here in this room.

"I don't know," he said at last. For a moment he was disheartened. What was the point to growing up if then you mostly just sat in the room? On the other hand—he cheered up—on the other hand, you could, if you wished, stay up all night every night. Nobody could *ever* tell you when to go to bed.

And tonight nobody was going to tell him.

"That was a nice birthday," he said. "That was just about the nicest birthday I ever had." He thought a moment. "I'm ever having, I mean. I'm going right on having it, aren't I?"

"So you are," said Mr. Davis. "Very well, it says on your itinerary that reasonable requests will be granted. Would you care to make a reasonable request, sir?"

"I'd like to be read to," Marshall said promptly. "And then I'd like to have another piece of cake." He hesitated because he knew there was only one piece left.

"That's all right," said Mrs. Davis. "It's your birthday cake, and you should certainly have the last piece."

So Marshall settled down in the big chair on his father's lap with a library book. Fudge came and settled on Marshall's lap, and the adventures of *Stuart Little* were picked up from where they'd left off last time. They had gotten to where Stuart becomes a substitute teacher, when Mr. Davis began to clear his throat. But then there did not come the closing of the book and the "That's all for tonight, Marshall; we'll go on with this tomorrow."

There was simply a switch in readers. Mrs. Davis took over and on they went. . . .

They finished that book and might have started another except that Marshall began to think about the cake waiting in the kitchen. After cake and milk he remembered that there had also been, in what Franny had read aloud to him, a part about walking in Greenwich Village after bedtime.

"Could we go for the walk now?" he asked.

"By all means," said Mr. Davis. "We shall have to leave your mother behind, as she has to stay with Franny and Jimmy."

"Oh, yes," said Marshall. "We couldn't leave the children alone, could we?"

Even at this terribly late hour the streets of Greenwich Village were crowded. There were a lot of children. Some of them, Marshall decided, even younger than he was. They darted among the grown-ups, yelling, laughing, playing games, darting out in the street and back. Some were crying. Some were sitting or standing by themselves, saying nothing, doing nothing. Marshall grew thoughtful.

"Why are *they* up, Papa? Do some kids get to stay up all night every night?" He tugged a bit desperately at his father's hand.

Mr. Davis, looking rather stern, said, "Perhaps they do, Marshall. Maybe they go out or stay in or go to bed or stay up just as they please because nobody cares what they do."

"Oh."

They walked on. In a little while Marshall squeezed his father's hand and skipped a little. "Could we get the fifteen cents worth of refreshment now?" he asked.

Mr. Davis blinked. "Marshall, you've been eating for hours. You mean you want to eat more?"

"Yes. Popcorn, I think."

They bought a bag of popcorn. It was snowy and golden and smelled delicious. Marshall didn't see how anyone could resist it. But Papa did. Papa, in fact, when they got back upstairs, sat in his big chair and said he'd just close his eyes for a minute here. Just for a minute. He was asleep almost immediately.

Marshall turned indignantly to his mother, who smiled and said, "Papa's had a tiring, exciting day. We'll just let him rest for a bit. What would you like to do now?"

"Could we play Go Fish?" Marshall asked, bouncing up to get the cards.

They did that for quite a while. It was fun sitting at the kitchen table with Mama, shouting in a whisper when he caught a card, catching more and more of them.

Fudge, who had been given a piece of popcorn too, played with it around their feet, finally settled down to eat it, his head tipped to one side. Then he went to the closed door of the children's room and scratched at the sill, turning to meow a demand.

"It appears that he wants to go to bed," said Mrs. Davis in a lazy voice.

"Without me?"

"I guess he's given up on you. And he doesn't need you to be sleepy, he just knows that he is. Shall we let him in there?"

"All right," Marshall said slowly. He did think that Fudge could have stayed up on this important night. First Papa, now Fudge . . .

"Cats need their sleep the same as all the rest of us," said Mama.

"I don't," Marshall said firmly.

"I'm beginning to believe it." Mrs. Davis got up and softly opened the bedroom door a crack so that Fudge could slip in and put himself to bed in the bottom bunk.

"Come, sit here on the sofa with me," Mrs. Davis said quietly. Marshall settled beside her, and Papa went right on sleeping.

"Shall I tell you some stories?" he whispered.

"That would be nice."

So Marshall, remembering to talk softly, told a story about a boy and his pet fire engine that followed him all over and tried to climb the stairs to the apartment where the boy lived and wailed its siren whenever the boy went away. The story ended with the boy and his whole family going to live in the firehouse. Then he told one about a boy and his pet lion, and another about a boy and his pet dragon. Then, for variety, he told one about a dancing mermaid, but it wasn't a very good story, since he was uncertain on the subject of mermaids. After he'd told a dozen or twenty stories, he asked his mother if she wanted a turn to tell some.

She said of course; and she told one about a mother owl getting all the little owls tucked away in their nest for the night, and after she'd got them all tucked in the mother owl was going to . . . was going to . . . Her voice got softer . . . and slower . . . and trailed away. . . .

Marshall turned to look, and there was Mama—asleep.

He got up carefully and stood by himself in the middle of the room, looking all around. He looked at his father, slumped in the big chair, and then at his mother, leaning back on the sofa, and then at the closed door behind which Franny, Fudge, and Jimmy were all asleep.

There was no sound at all, inside or out, except his own low breathing and an automobile horn far off now and then and the ticking of the kitchen clock.

Marshall tiptoed to the sideboard and studied the clock. The hands weren't exactly *on* anything, so he couldn't tell what time it was. He poured a glass of milk and ate the rest of the popcorn. After that he remained in the kitchen, sitting on a chair tipped back against the wall, blowing softly on his plastic ocarina.

Some time later, sort of stiff but not uncomfortable, he found himself leaning forward instead, sort of resting on the table top. The plastic ocarina was on the floor beside him.

He stretched and yawned and was glad he hadn't fallen asleep. But maybe, he admitted, he'd had "a wink or two," as Papa liked to say.

He went back in the living room, and as he looked from his mother to his father the bells of St. Anthony of Padua began to ring out. First they played a tune, then they struck the hour. Marshall set his mind to count.

One . . . two . . . three . . . four . . . five . . .

They stopped.

Five o'clock.

It was morning, and he had been up all night. At the window a faint grayness had replaced the dark and there was the sound of waking in the street at the end of the alley. An alarm clock went off someplace.

Marshall yawned long and hugely, smiled, and went into the bedroom. He got into the bottom bunk and dragged the covers up. Fudge moved over a little to make room, then curled in the crook of Marshall's knees, but Franny and Jim didn't stir.

"I *told* you," Marshall whispered. "I told you that people on their birthdays have parties and presents and cakes and—things. Lots of things. . . ."

Chapter Fourteen

Franny came into the cafeteria, carrying a brown paper bag with her lunch in it. She gave the teacher at the desk a bright, triumphant smile and marched down the rows of tables looking for Simone.

"Franny! Franny, over here!"

Franny drew a deep breath and almost laughed aloud with pleasure. Just that easily it was just like the olden times. She sat down beside her friend, drew from the bag a sandwich and an apple, arranging these before her with meticulous care but not immediately beginning to eat.

"Papa's got a job," she said.

"I know. Francisco told me."

"Papa says he believes in gestures. He says a gesture is the only thanks a man can make for his good fortune."

"He does? Has he made a gesture?"

"This is it," said Franny, indicating her lunch. "I'm going to carry my lunch to school from now on. I mean, Papa hasn't actually gotten paid yet or anything, so that's what makes it a gesture." She began to eat.

After a while Simone said, "Francisco is crazy about his job at the shoe store."

Franny nodded.

"It's funny, isn't it," Simone went on. "There's Francisco with your papa's other job, and because he has it, then your papa got another one, because of Mr. Wheeler looking at the picture and all and then getting a job for your papa. Francisco says Mr. Wheeler has connections."

"I guess he does, all right."

"What's the job?" Simone asked.

Franny swallowed the last of her sandwich. "Well, it's in an advertising agency, only I don't know what doing except that Papa says he can stand it. The trouble with all the other jobs he had was he couldn't stand them. Only I don't think that's what he's thanking his good fortune for." She picked up her apple and turned it slowly, admiring its striped beauty. "Mr. Wheeler likes Papa's paintings, and he's going to put one in his art gallery, and that's what's making Papa so happy. And Mama," she added. "And us."

Lila Wembleton came up to them. "Can I sit here?" she said and plumped her blue lunch box on the table. "I mean, is it all *right?*"

She sounded, Franny thought, stuck-up and not stuck-up all at the same time. Like somebody who hadn't decided how to be. Or didn't know how to be.

"It's okay with me," said Franny as Simone was saying, "Sure, why not?"

"Since when are you two friends again?" said Lila. "I mean, I thought you'd had this terrible quarrel and all."

Simone and Franny looked at each other and then at Lila. They shook their heads.

"We didn't quarrel," said Franny.

"Not really," said Simone.

"Oh." Lila fussed around in her lunch box and said, not looking up, "Well, then, maybe you both would come to my house on Sunday? I *mean,* we could play records and all, and talk. I mean, if you'd *like* to."

What she sounds like, Franny realized, because

she knew the feeling well, what she sounds like is somebody who wants to be friends but isn't sure anyone is going to want to be friends back.

"I think that'd be nice," she said, looking at Simone, who nodded. "I think it'd be very nice." She almost added from force of habit, If I can bring Marshall, and then remembered that Francisco was going to take Marshall and the Orgella boys all the way up to Central Park on Sunday.

She found, and didn't feel the least bit guilty about it, that she was looking forward to some time without Marshall, now that he was five and no longer a baby. Because there just are times, she said to herself, when girls should be able to get together just by themselves, and play records and talk and talk. . . .

She could hardly wait.